THE PRICE OF GETTING INVOLVED

They were all over Ruel like a wolf pack. One man dove at his legs. Ruel hit him on the back of the neck with the heel of his hand. Someone grabbed him from behind, tripping him. As he fell, carrying the fellow down with him, something hard and heavy hit him on the temple.

He lay for a moment, unable to move, trying to get his eyes into focus. Frank Gant came over to him and kicked him, with all the force he could muster, in the ribs.

Ruel came to his feet, growling like any hurt animal, and ran at the man. Frank Gant stepped aside, grinning. Why don't you quit this? a voice inside Ruel said. All you'll get is a beating. He felt a hard contempt for himself. He hit Frank Gant on the neck, and then he was on the ground, with no clear idea of how he had got there.

"Had enough?" Frank Gant asked him.

Somehow the question roused an iron stubbornness in Ruel. He thought: "You better kill me, Gant. I'll get you for this if you don't."

The big man kicked him again. He had a feeling of falling endlessly, and then he had no feeling. . . .

Other Avon Books by
Richard Brister

WOLF STREAK   15321 $.75

CAT EYES

RICHARD BRISTER

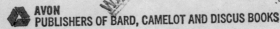 **AVON**
PUBLISHERS OF BARD, CAMELOT AND DISCUS BOOKS

CAT EYES is an original publication of Avon Books.

AVON BOOKS
A division of
The Hearst Corporation
959 Eighth Avenue
New York, New York 10019

Copyright © 1973 by Richard Brister
Published by arrangement with the author.
ISBN: 0-380-01784-9

First Avon Printing, May, 1973.
Third Printing

AVON TRADEMARK REG. U.S. PAT. OFF. AND
FOREIGN COUNTRIES, REGISTERED TRADEMARK—
MARCA REGISTRADA, HECHO EN CHICAGO, U.S.A.

Printed in the U.S.A.

To Kay, again.

1

The rifle in the rocks spoke again. From where he sat his horse halfway up the mountain, Ruel Matheson could hear a resounding *thwack* as the slug found its target, a barrel-shaped water wagon lumbering along the floor of the basin.

Water squirted from the wagon side where the bullet had entered. The girl on the high wagon seat glanced up the slope toward the rocks where the sniper lay hidden.

Ruel's dun horse flung his head around as if to say, "Let's get out of here." Ruel laid his hand on the animal's neck, which was slick and shiny with sweat.

"Easy, boy," he said.

The rifle sounded again. The girl rein-whipped her oxen, trying to put herself and the wagon beyond rifle range. The oxen refused to be hurried.

Don't guess they mind bein' shot at, Ruel thought. He felt sympathy for the girl, who didn't look to be much more than out of her teens.

A tendril of smoke curled up from the rocks, pinpointing the sniper's position. Ruel swore, watching the man, who lay behind an imbedded, cinder-like stone of volcanic origin, lift his rifle to his cheek and shoot again. He would hit the girl, if he wasn't careful.

Ruel studied the mountainside, noting several ravines, and a stand of piñon that clung to a gravel slope. If he chose to, he could probably cat-foot it down there without showing himself to the sniper.

He thought about it a moment. Then his eyes took on an expression of flinty withdrawal. He urged his horse up the slope.

He tried to ignore the shooting below, which went on

7

with idiotic persistence. After some minutes, with the resigned air of a man letting himself in for trouble, he climbed down and tethered the dun in a clump of bullberry.

He drew his carbine out of its crude, homemade sling, levered a cartridge into firing position, and picked his way down toward the rocks—a tall, awkward-seeming man whose awkwardness was only apparent, who moved with deceptive, ungainly grace, like some large animal of the jungle.

He took ten minutes, keeping always to cover, to reach the rocks. He knelt behind a granite upthrust, lifted the carbine, and drew a bead on the sniper, whose attention was riveted on the girl and her wagon.

"You make a habit of shootin' at girls?" Ruel asked, speaking just loudly enough to be heard.

The man didn't move. He said, without turning his head, "Who wants to know?"

"Put that rifle down," Ruel said.

"Why should I?"

"I've got a carbine trained on you. I'm in no friendly mood."

The man set the rifle on a rock slab beside him and rolled over to a sitting position. He was a chunky customer with bloodless lips and pale-blue, dead-looking eyes in a pocked face. His collarless calico shirt, under a salt-and-pepper vest, was a rich dirty gray at the neckband. The only clean thing about him was the Bull Durham tag dangling from his vest pocket.

He wore his gun tied down, Ruel noticed, in an oiled, flapless holster.

"Get up," Ruel said, picking his way down to the fellow. "Keep your hands away from your body where I can see them."

"How'd you get in so close?" The man's eyes, as he rose, crinkled at Ruel. A faint contempt glimmered in them. "What are you, some kind of breed Injun?"

Ruel scowled at that question. His Kiowa blood was apparent, he knew, in his shallowly socketed eyes and in his hair, which was black and inclined to be stringy. And it was none of this fellow's damned business.

"Turn around, friend. Face away from me. Use your left hand to unbuckle the belt."

The pock-faced man grinned. He glanced down the slope, his eyes focused on a dirt road that snaked along through the foothills, and his grin widened.

Ruel said. "This funny to you?"

"Sure."

You're pretty happy for a man in your fix, Ruel thought, eying the man with misgiving. How come you're so happy?

He thumbcocked the carbine. "Take the belt off, friend."

The man, as he let his holstered gun fall, pulled his lips back at Ruel, exposing ferret-like teeth.

"Where's your horse?" Ruel asked.

"Over in them trees. Why?"

Ruel gestured with the carbine. "Let's get him."

"What about my hardware?" the man grumbled. "That's a forty-four forty Winchester layin' on the ground." Ruel shrugged, and the man said, "I want to know what you're aimin' to do."

"Do you?"

The man was silent, studying Ruel. "You don't scare me none with that carbine."

"Don't I?"

"No. You know why?"

"Why?"

"I don't figure you'll use it. You never saw me before. You got no idea what this is about. You're probably wishin' you'd never took cards in the game."

Ruel brought the carbine up deliberately and squeezed the trigger, putting a neat small hole through the crown of the man's hat, an old black sombrero whose brim had been slit and threaded with rawhide to keep it from sagging. The man swept the hat off his head. His pale eyes came up, blazing.

"I oughtta kill you for that."

"I can come closer," Ruel said. "Move, unless you want a lead haircut."

The man regarded him, gauging his temper, then forced a smile with killing anger behind it and turned, walking toward the tangle of trees in which he claimed to have left his horse. There was something casual, too unconcerned, Ruel thought, in the man's manner.

It took half an hour to pick up their two horses and ride down to where the girl had halted the water-wagon alongside a rickety windmill. With the help of a cowpuncher who'd been nowhere in sight a few minutes ago, she was transferring what remained of her cargo to a galvanized iron trough.

A dozen gaunt steers, wearing a C Bar brand, crowded around, poking their noses into the trough, sucking up the precious, life-giving liquid.

The girl regarded Ruel without friendliness. Ruel inclined his head toward his riding companion. "You know this fellow, ma'am?"

"I know him." She wore scuffed halfboots and a floppy, wide-brimmed man's hat, there was a smudge on her cheek, and still Ruel's pulse quickened as he looked at her.

"My name's Matheson, ma'am," he said, touching his hat. "I thought you might like a closer look at this jasper."

"I'm Jean Wright." She indicated the cowpuncher. "This is Woody Yarmon. I appreciate your trying to help, but I wish you hadn't. I wasn't in any real danger."

"Oh?" Ruel said.

Woody Yarmon, a stocky, sober young man who appeared to carry the weight of the world on his shoulders, inclined his head toward the pock-faced man. "He wouldn't have hit her."

"No?" Ruel said.

The cowpuncher looked at him, not smiling, very serious about this. "Don't you know who he is?"

"Who?"

"Harry McLouth."

The pock-faced man perked up as his name was mentioned. His eyes shifted toward Ruel. Can't wait to see if I've heard of you, can you? Ruel thought.

He'd heard of him. A few years ago, according to Ruel's information, this man McLouth had fallen out with the only friend he ever had. After badgering him into a gunfight, he'd killed him. He'd made a name for himself since then as a gunman. Only six months ago, in Tombstone, he had shot it out with the notorious Bagley brothers, and had killed the pair of them.

McLouth, grinning easily now, leaned forward to gather up his reins.

"Be seein' you," he said.

"Hold it," Ruel said.

"Not me," said the gunman. "I'm ridin'."

"On the strength of your name, eh?" Ruel said, looking into the killer's pale eyes.

"Please," the girl said, "don't get in any deeper with him than you are."

"I can handle him," Ruel said. He tilted the carbine, letting McLouth stare down its muzzle. McLouth eased back in the saddle. He eyed Ruel a bleak instant, then he shrugged and sat grinning.

Ruel spoke to the girl. "What's this all about, ma'am?"

She indicated McLouth. "The man he works for—Frank Gant—is trying to force my dad to sell C Bar to him. He's dammed the creek that runs through his place on its way down to ours. We've taken him into court, but you know how slow the law is. We're still waiting for a ruling."

Ruel glanced at the scrawny animals standing dejectedly around the now empty trough. Heat waves shimmered out on the flat; the short, tawny buffalo grass was dry and crackly as hay. No rain had fallen hereabouts lately.

"You say he's dammed the creek. Why don't you pull his dam down, ma'am?"

McLouth grinned at Ruel's question. The girl let her cowpuncher friend answer for her.

"Frank Gant has more'n a dozen men workin' for him," Woody Yarmon said. "At C Bar there's only her father and me."

Ruel took out makings and fashioned a cigarette. He struck a match on the inside of his boot, where contact with stirrup leather had worn it smooth. This fellow Gant was probably drunk on power. There might be more to the story, but on the basis of what he'd been told he did not like Frank Gant, Ruel decided.

11

"How hard up are you for water?" he asked Woody Yarmon.

"We got one windmill still pumping. The well at our headquarters is producing. That's it now. Jean's been distributin' what water we have around the range."

"While our friend here," Ruel said, "amuses himself shooting at her."

"He wasn't shooting at me," Jean said.

"What's it take to rile you, ma'am?" Ruel asked.

"I know you want to help," the girl said. "But really, I can take care of myself." She smiled at him as she picked up her reins. "I appreciate the trouble you've taken."

As Ruel touched his hat, the girl's eyes met his full on.

"Be careful," she said, flicking a glance toward McLouth.

Ruel acknowledged the warning with a crooked smile. She shook her reins at the oxen. The empty wagon lurched away, Woody Yarmon keeping pace with it on horseback. The girl handled the reins, Ruel noticed, as authoritatively as a man. She's a spunky little somebody, he thought. And as easy to look at as sunshine on water.

McLouth brought him back from woolgathering. "Kind of leaves you holdin' a tiger by the tail, don't it?"

Ruel turned toward the gunfighter. "You bein' the tiger, I take it?"

McLouth leaned forward and spat down along his horse's left foreleg. He wiped his mouth with the back of a grimy hand. "Sure."

"Let's get something straight, McLouth," Ruel said.

"What?"

"I've seen gunfighters. Your kind doesn't scare me."

"No?"

"No."

McLouth's pale eyes glittered. "When I've got my gun back I may do somethin' about that."

Ruel frowned, wondering what it was in a man that made him act so tough. He said after a moment, "I saw rooftops eastward from up on the ridge. What town would that be?"

"Chenango. Why?"

"Chenango," Ruel said. He looked up. "Is there any kind of John Law in Chenango?"

"Sure. There's a marshal. What about it?"

Ruel brought his horse fiddlefooting around, heading him toward the town. "We'll let the law decide what's to be done with you," he said.

McLouth gave him a flat stare, grinned, and gigged his horse forward. They rode along at a trot, leaving the basin floor presently to follow a dug road that snaked along through the foothills.

They passed a deserted shanty knocked half awry by the wind, with only a few poles remaining to mark where its corral had been, its windmill long since reduced to rubble. A jackrabbit scampered up a ravine, acting scarier, Ruel felt, than he had any right to. Overhead, against a slatey sky, a hawk coasted. There was something ominous in the air. Ruel didn't like the looks of this country.

McLouth's pocked face, he saw, wore an expression of amused expectancy. What's he smiling about? Ruel thought.

2

He had an answer sooner than he expected. The click of a horse's hoof against stone brought his head around; he saw a big, hard-looking man ride out from a tangle of brush at the roadside. Three more men emerged from the brush. All four of them came clattering up the road, grinning at some joke only they knew the point of.

One of the latecomers, a paunchy man with a bulbous nose in a blotchy red face, greeted Ruel.

Ruel acknowledged it with a nod. The man spoke to McLouth. "Where you goin', Harry?"

"Chenango." McLouth indicated Ruel with a flick of his eyes. "This damn breed Injun says he's gunna turn me in to the marshal."

"Why, that ain't nice. That's downright mean of him," the man with the paunch said.

The big man who'd led these men up here said, "Cass?" The paunchy man said, "Yeah?" and the big man said, "Shut up."

The man spoken to swallowed, and lapsed into an uneasy silence. The big man, who was almost overpoweringly handsome, with hard gray eyes and an aggressive cleft chin, turned toward McLouth.

"How'd he get the drop on you?"

McLouth glanced at Ruel. "Damn if I know. He come up on me out of nowhere. If he made any sound, I never heard it. One minute I'm lobbin' slugs into C Bar's water wagon, next thing I know this joker's got his carbine trained on me. There wasn't anything I could do."

The big man studied Ruel. "Anybody ever tell you it pays to mind your own business?"

"Sure."

14

"Why'd you stick your nose into mine?"

"When a girl's bein' shot at, I figure it's my business."

The big man's eyes glinted. "You any idea whose toe you've trod on? There's only one outfit worthy of the name in this country. That's my Y Lightning. My name's Gant—Frank Gant. I run this country."

Ruel rubbed the back of his neck. "Don't seem like, if a man's all that big and important, he'd take the trouble to brag about it."

There was a silence during which Frank Gant's men looked at the tops of their horses' heads, at the sky, at the ground, anywhere but at their employer, whose face had turned blotchy red. Ruel heard a creak of saddle leather behind. He turned his head as one of the Y Lightning riders swung at him with the heavy end of a quirt.

Ruel blocked the blow with an uplifted arm. A loop dropped around him and tightened, pinning his arms to his sides, dragging him from the saddle. He managed to hit the ground on his feet, but the man on the business end of the rope spurred his horse, dragging Ruel down and along the road.

One of Frank Gant's men ran alongside, relieving him of his gun, after which he was permitted to stand and shake free of the rope.

He stood with his hands on his hips, regarding the big man, who had climbed down off his claybank stud.

"I don't hear so good," the big man grinned. "What were you sayin' before you and your horse parted company?"

I'm supposed to eat my words now, Ruel thought. "The gist of it'd be that a man who's got anything to brag about doesn't need to brag," he said.

The big man's jaw tightened. "You don't seem to've learned anything, buster."

"What was I supposed to learn?" Ruel asked.

The big man slapped him hard on the face. Ruel's right arm, having been used to fend off that quirt, was of little use to him. He made the big man wince with a short, hooking left, and he was boring in, carrying the fight to his heavier opponent, when one of the Y Lightning riders leaped on him from behind.

15

He could feel the man's forearm biting into his Adam's apple, cutting off his breath. He bent low, hurling the man off his back in a spraddle-legged somersault, and dropped his hand toward his empty holster as the others closed in. He brought his hands up and faced them.

"All right," he said. "Come and get it, you sons of bitches."

None of them, suddenly, seemed to want to come to grips with him. Frank Gant said, "Get him. Don't let him bluff you."

They were all over Ruel then like a wolf pack. One man dove at his legs. Ruel hit him on the back of the neck with the heel of his hand, felt the clinging arms slip away. Someone grabbed him from behind, tripping him. As he fell, carrying the fellow down with him, something hard and heavy hit him on the temple.

He lay for a moment unable to move, trying to get his eyes into focus. Frank Gant came over to him and kicked him, with all the force he could muster, in the ribs.

Ruel came to his feet, growling like any hurt animal, and ran at the man. Frank Gant stepped aside, grinning. He drove his hand into Ruel's body.

Ruel hit back, poking Frank Gant on the nose with his left, using his injured right to feint the big man off-balance. He found Frank's nose again with the left. The big man cursed and waved his men aside. There was something wild, unstable in his eyes as he closed with Ruel.

Why don't you quit this? a voice inside Ruel said. All you'll get is a beating. He felt a hard contempt for himself. He struck out at Frank Gant's contorted face.

The big man hit him on the mouth, cutting him, not knocking him down, not trying to, Ruel sensed! He moved stubbornly forward, trying to get inside, away from this man's cunning fists.

He hit Frank Gant on the neck, and then he was on the ground, with no clear idea how he had got there.

Frank Gant stood over him, nudging him with a booted foot. "Get up. I ain't through with you yet."

Ruel rose, striking out feebly, ineffectively with his right hand. He was knocked down again. And now came the nightmare. He seemed to spend hours being knocked down, getting up, and being knocked down again. He lost consciousness several times, only to be jolted awake by a kick, and the sight of Frank Gant standing over him.

"Had enough?" the big man kept asking.

Somehow that question roused an iron stubbornness in Ruel. He rose dazedly to his hands and knees, and was kicked down again.

He tried to bring the Y Lightning owner into focus. He thought, you better kill me, Gant. I'll get you for this if you don't.

The big man kicked him again. He had a feeling of falling endlessly, and then he had no feeling.

3

Frank Gant, when he saw that the man on the ground was unconscious, kicked him again. His anger, now that he had no object for it, subsided. He stepped back, his chest heaving.

His men stared at him. They were a little shocked at the way he'd let temper take him, Frank saw, and he smiled. Except for Red Coombs, Frank's foreman, there wasn't a man of the lot who hadn't a notch or two in his gun. McLouth was reputed to have killed six men.

Red Coombs gave a wondering shake of his head as he regarded the man on the ground.

"By God, he never quit," Red said. "That's a lot of man lyin' there, Frank."

Frank shrugged.

McLouth said, "He ain't tough," adding, as Red opened his mouth to protest, "He's out cold, ain't he?"

"Only because we were too many for him," said the foreman. "You ask me, he put up one helluva fight for a man with a bunged-up arm and a lump the size of an egg on his forehead." The redheaded man turned toward Frank. "Who d' you suppose he is?"

"I don't know and I don't give a damn," Frank said. He watched Lute Springer kneel beside the unconscious man and probe for the pulse. "Well?" Frank said. "What about it?"

"His heart's just about beatin'." Lute Springer bent to examine the lump on Ruel Matheson's forehead. "Maybe I shouldn't've used my gun on him," he said.

"Why did you?" Frank asked.

"I figured if I knocked him cold I might save him from

a beating. He's a hard man to knock out though. Why'd you kick him when he was out, Frank?"

"The son of a bitch refused to say 'Uncle'."

"How in hell could he?" Lute asked. "He didn't know what he was doin'."

He knew, Frank thought. Why didn't he quit? Any other man would have. He stared with unappeased anger at the man on the ground, wondering what to do about him now. His mouth clamped. He waved his men toward their horses. They climbed to saddle like dutiful dogs, all except Lute, who stayed with the hurt man.

"What about him, Frank?"

"What about him?"

Lute's eyes fell away from Frank's. He dragged a foot through the dirt. He'd had a Christian upbringing; his father'd been a back-country preacher somewhere in Missouri. "We can't ride off and leave him here, Frank."

"Why can't we?"

"He's hurt. More'n you realize."

"And your heart bleeds for him, don't it?" Frank asked.

Some of the others snickered at that. Lute's face turned red. He stood there, unable to think of anything to say. Frank broke a long silence, asking, "You ridin' with us, Lute?"

Lute Springer looked at the man on the ground, then up at Frank. He opened his mouth, and closed it.

"Make up your mind," Frank said. "Make up your mind, Lute."

After another long moment of indecision, Lute Springer caught up his horse's reins and lifted himself to the saddle. Frank slapped his claybank to motion. His men, all but McLouth, who had a rifle to fetch from up on the mountain, followed a respectful few yards behind.

When, an hour later, they pulled up in Y Lightning's yard, Frank climbed down creakily and handed his reins to Lute.

"Turn him down into the pasture."

Lute's face was sullen as he led the horse away. Have to beat some of that wrongheadedness out of Lute, Frank thought, as he entered Y Lightning's old log-and-masonry house.

He hung his hat on the wall peg inside the heavy oaken door, and moved on into a living room decorated with the heads of deer, elk, moose, bear, bobcat, and bison. He never tired of these trophies, all of which he'd bagged with his .50 Winchester, using the 110-grain charge and the hollow-point, 300-grain bullet.

His mother glanced up from the alcove, where she sat mending a tear in Frank's spare Levis.

"Why don't you sit over there and be comfortable?" Frank said, indicating his upholstered chair by the window.

His mother peered at him over the rims of her glasses. "I feel more comfortable here." She glanced up at Frank's gallery of stuffed heads, and her mouth twitched. "All those staring eyes are enough to give a body goose pimples."

She went on sewing, a tiny woman whose highboned face and taut skin gave her the appearance of a cadaver. Frank watched her send the needle flicking in and out through the cloth of his Levis, his skin crawling at the thought that such a creature had whelped him.

"You needn't have bothered to mend that."

"I like having something to do, Frank. By the way—" she pointed at a shiny black object on her sewing table "—this was in your trousers' pocket."

"Levis," Frank said. "The word out here is Levis."

"Levis, trousers, what's the difference? That's coal, isn't it?" Frank nodded reluctantly, and she said, "How can you keep any pockets when you carry such truck in them, Frank? What would you want with a piece of coal, anyway?"

Frank, cursing her for her curiosity, said, "It's a memento."

"Memento? Of what? Don't tell me you carry this to remind you what your father did for a living?"

Frank shook his head, his mouth twisting.

"You needn't make a face. Somebody has to dig the world's coal, Frank."

"I suppose." He took the coal off the table and hefted it, grinning. He'd found it a year ago, while stalking a seven-point buck on the low ridge that formed the north boundary of Lucas Wright's C Bar range. After poking about up there for an hour he'd located a seam of anthracite eight feet thick, extending God-knows-how-far into the mountain, and he had been drunk with excitement.

Let fools scrabble for gold. Frank would take coal. As a miner's son he had served his own brief apprenticeship underground. He knew enough about such things to be convinced that the coal on C Bar's ridge could be taken out at a profit.

He envisioned a town in a crease of the mountain—a town and a stately mansion staring down at the shanty houses of the miners.

My mansion, Frank thought. My miners. My town. Call it Gantville. Or maybe Gant City'd have a more substantial sound to it.

That was his dream. The key to his dream, the means of its achievement, was possession of C Bar. Somehow, without appearing to want it greatly, he must gain title to Lucas Wright's land. Lucas, so far, had refused to sell to him. I'll bring him around, Frank thought.

His mother was waiting for him to explain that piece of coal in his pocket. He gave a moment's thought to the problem.

"In case you're forgetting," he said, "I used to deal faro in a saloon."

His mother registered disapproval by frowning, as always when Frank mentioned this subject. "I'm aware of it, Frank. What does that have to do with—"

"Gamblers are a superstitious lot," Frank said. "We all went in for luck charms, one kind or another." He looked at his mother and grinned. "I knew a man who lived with a whore for six months because she brought him luck at the tables. When his luck ran out, he cut her off like a hangnail."

"If you don't mind, I'd as soon not hear such things, Frank," his mother said primly.

Frank wondered how she'd react if she knew the man he'd told her about was himself. Hefting the coal in his hand, he said, "I picked this up nine years ago stepping down off the train in Stobie, Montana. I was damn near

21

broke when I hit that town. Two days later I'd won a thousand dollars playing stud with a pair of old mossy-horns who thought they were sharpers. That thousand was my first real stake. I've come a long way up the hill since I picked this coal up. Maybe it's been lucky for me. Maybe it hasn't. But I don't intend to part with it."

His mother wagged her head at him, mild reproof in her eyes. She'd swallowed it, Frank saw. He turned away from her, grinning. Later, standing at the window of his own room, he stared across miles of undulating grass and sage toward C Bar's mountain.

He could see again, in his mind's eye, the seam of coal he'd found up in there. When a seam like that surfaced there had to be, as Frank saw it, millions of dollars worth of the stuff underground. At the thought of so much money, greed rose up in him like a sickness. I'll kill Lucas Wright, he thought, if he don't come around.

He pulled his boots off and lay on the bed, thinking of Lucas's girl, who would be alone in the world if he killed her father. But not long though—not a fancy little pack-age like that one. He wondered if there could be any truth to the talk going around about her and that fool, Woody Yarmon.

Remembering how Jean Wright had tongue-lashed him after he'd dammed Whitewoman Creek and cut off C Bar's primary source of water, Frank grinned. He'd had an almost uncontrollable urge to shut her mouth with a kiss that day. What would have happened, he wondered, if he had tried that? It wasn't as if he were some kind of gorilla. He'd always made out with the women. Some that started out hating him had wound up in bed with him. That girl's got her instincts, he thought, same as all the rest of them. All I'd have to do is catch her at the right time and push the right buttons.

He fell asleep. Oddly, he didn't dream of the girl, but of the man he'd kicked and beaten to unconsciousness down there by C Bar. In his dream he kept knocking the fellow down until his arm grew so tired he could no longer lift it. His arm fell off and lay on the ground at his feet. The stranger named Matheson bent to pick Frank's arm up and was about to hit him with it when Frank woke up, sweating.

He swabbed his face and neck with a towel, and after pulling into his boots tramped outside in a foul frame of mind. He found his mother on the patio having a quiet, apparently serious talk with Lute Springer.

"When'd you two get so clubby?" Frank growled.

"I understand you beat a man within an inch of his life, Frank, and left him in the road."

Frank lowered his brows at Lute Springer. "You been shootin' your mouth off?"

"There's no point in being angry at Luther, Frank. I wormed this out of him. How could you do such a thing? Don't you care what happens to that poor—"

"This ain't Pennsylvania," Frank said. "We got different ways out here than you're used to."

"I still don't see how you could leave a man in such condition."

"He got in my way," Frank said. "He stuck his nose in my business."

His mother looked at him as if he were some kind of reptile. "That's no reason to try to kill a man. Luther, ride out there and see what you can do to help him."

Lute's eyes came up at Frank's, then skittered away. As Lute started across the yard toward the corral, Frank said, "Lute?" in a cool, even voice. Lute Springer halted as abruptly as if he'd been snared by a catchrope.

"Yeah?" he said, turning.

"Where do you think you're going?"

The old woman said, "Luther, you go on." Frank wheeled on her, trembling.

"Shut up," he said.

His mother drew herself up. "Is that the way you speak to your mother?"

"I'll speak a damn sight plainer'n that if you don't close your trap," Frank said.

The old woman lifted a hand to her bony, cadaverous face. She was frightened now, Frank saw. He took hold of Lute's arm, dragged the man across the patio and around back of the house.

"All right," he said, "lets get straight on somethin'."

"Who you workin' for, Lute her or me?"

"You. But it don't go down with me, Frank, usin' a man the way we used that drifter."

Frank hit the smaller man on the jaw. Lute, running backward in an effort to keep his balance, tripped and fell to the ground. He propped himself on an elbow and looked up in sullen anger.

"How's that go down with you?"

Lute stood up, fingering the welt on his chin. All his anger seemed to melt away now as he faced Frank. "That ain't no way to treat a man."

"You can quit if you don't like it."

Lute's mouth slacked. His eyes went wide. "Who said anything about quittin'?"

"I did," Frank said. "I get the feelin' you're not happy here. No point in stickin' around, if workin' for this outfit makes you unhappy."

"I ain't unhappy."

Frank looked at him in a cold, impersonal way.

"You got me all wrong, Frank."

"Have I?"

"Maybe I spoke out of turn. I never meant nothing by it. Sometimes my temper runs away with my tongue."

"I don't like a man usin' his temper on me. I don't put up with it."

"It won't happen again, Frank." Lute had the look of a scolded dog.

"You're right it won't," Frank said.

"I ain't quittin' this outfit," Lute said. "Where would I go if I did?"

Frank gave him a few seconds to think about it, then said, "You like workin' for Y Lightnin'."

"Sure." Lute's smile was ingratiating. "Who wouldn't?"

"I pay you a fightin' man's pay," Frank said. "What makes you think you're worth it?"

Lute frowned. "You mean because my old man preached the gospel?"

"I mean you're too squeamish."

Lute slapped his holstered gun. "I ain't squeamish when the lead starts flyin'. Give me a chance, Frank."

24

Frank turned his head, coughed, and smiled into his lifted hand.

"I'll expect you to keep away from my mother from now on."

"Sure, Frank. Whatever you say."

"I want Lucas Wright's land. One way or another I'm goin' to have it. *If* you get my meanin'."

"That's all right. That's your business," Lute said.

"And yours. From here on in anybody's workin' for me'd better have a strong stomach." Frank dismissed the man with a curt, contemptuous nod and walked around to the front of the house.

He found his mother in the living room reading her Bible. She always ran to "the Good Book," when things went wrong for her. She marked her place with a bony, liver-spotted forefinger, and glanced up as Frank entered. Her hesitant smile suggested that if he wanted to patch up their quarrel she would meet him halfway.

Frank stared stonily at her. He bit the end off a cigar and settled into his chair. His mother waited until he'd struck a match to the stogie before she spoke to him. "I hope you weren't too hard on Luther."

Frank tilted his head back and blew a smoke ring at the ceiling.

"You didn't fire him, did you, Frank?"

"What's it to you?"

His mother stared at him, feigning shock at his rudeness. "I feel responsible, in a way."

"Don't," Frank said. "Just quit nosin' in things that don't concern you."

"You're my son, Frank. Anything you do concerns me."

"Hell," Frank said.

His mother wagged her head, as though to say his case was hopeless. "I think I'll pray for you tonight, Frank."

"Don't bother." He saw her traplike mouth open. "Get off my back. Try to keep your mouth shut, why don't you?"

His mother looked away, holding her tongue, for a wonder. Frank, having asked for silence, found it oppressive. A fire was set in the fireplace, he saw. He struck a match to the crumpled newspapers. The piñon logs kindled, filling the room with a resinous fragrance.

He carried his chair and the card table across to the hearth, and dealt himself a solitaire layout—flipping the cards down onto the table, for his mother's benefit, with a professional flourish.

He played the spade ace to the board, played the club five to the six of hearts, then started through the pack. As he turned the cards, he found himself thinking about the drifter. A tingling excitement, threaded with pleasure, ran through him at the memory of his fight with the fellow.

He wished now that he'd had no advantage, that there'd been just the two of them slugging it out. Frank liked a fight; he always had. He'd found a worthy adversary in that lanky, never-quit drifter. That fellow had courage.

Poor devil could freeze, easy as not, lying out there in the road. Thinking of it, Frank knocked ash off his cigar, and hitched himself closer to the fire.

4

A cold wind off the mountain whipped along the road, throwing dust and debris in Ruel Matheson's face. He had the gritty taste of dirt in his mouth.

He lay with one arm pinned under him, and he hurt all over. He spat out some dirt, coughed lightly, and winced at a knifelike pain in the ribs.

The sun had long since heeled down in the west. Already it was bitterly cold. Burn all day and freeze all night, Ruel thought, that's high country for you. I better come alive. I better get out of here, or here's where the buzzards'll find me, come morning.

He tried to sit up, and winced again and lay back with a groan, closing his eyes, not breathing for a long moment. I'm hurt bad, he thought. He must've broke half my ribs, kickin' me that way. Why'd I stick my neck out for that girl to begin with?

How come I don't mind the cold? They say when you're freezin', all you feel is a numbness. You get to where you don't give a damn.

His left hand lay on the ground in front of him. He flexed his fingers. They might as well have belonged to somebody else, he couldn't feel them. I'm freezin', all right. Well, there's worse ways to go. Now quit that, he told himself angrily. You're not licked. Man's never licked till he quits.

He went on flexing his fingers until they began to hurt, then he eased himself to a sitting position against a gnarled piñon. He sat in a kind of stupor, feeling blood run out of his head, trying not to faint.

He slacked down onto his elbows, and stared up mindlessly at the sky.

27

Look at those clouds up there, he thought. Wouldn't you think clouds that dark would have some rain in them? Maybe they do. It must rain sometime around here. That's all I need now, he thought, a good drenching. His mouth twisted.

His horse had found grass down the road, he saw, and was grazing idly. Ruel tried to whistle the animal to him, but his bruised lips wouldn't pucker. He spoke to the dun, called him by name, but his voice was weak. The animal stared curiously at him, then went on grazing.

Ruel grasped a low limb of the piñon and dragged himself to his feet. The ground swirled under him. He hung on, waiting for light-headedness to pass. He limped along the road and hooked one arm across the dun horse's withers. He could feel the sap running out of his legs. It was all he could do to stay on his feet, much less lift himself to the saddle.

Using the dun as a crutch, he moved down the road toward a brown-shale outcrop which could be made to serve, he saw, as a mounting block. He used up the last of his strength easing himself down off the shelf and into the saddle. Once there, he grasped the horn and shut his eyes, holding on like a man drowning.

For an instant now he permitted himself to think of the past, to reflect on what his life had been. The angry resolve of a man who feels that he has been cheated straightened him up momentarily. He felt himself sagging, and thought bitterly, I'm cooked. I can't ride fifty yards, the shape I'm in.

He cursed himself for entertaining such thoughts, and touched the dun with his bootheels. The animal carried him along the road.

Woody Yarmon had to keep pulling rein, adjusting his pace to that of Jean in the wagon. When finally C Bar's high, hip-roofed barn poked up over a rise, Jean's oxen broke into a lumbering run, and Woody free-reined his pony.

He couldn't get his mind off Harry McLouth, and the way the drifter, Matheson, had baited the killer.

That took nerve, Woody thought. 'Course, he had a

gun. I guess he felt safe enough, tellin' an unarmed man off. But somethin' tells me he'd've talked just as tough if McLouth had been packin' an iron.

The wagon rattled into the ranch yard. Lucas Wright came out of the house wearing a checked, red-and-white apron over his starboots and Levis.

"Dad," Jean called with a smile, "have you any idea how you look in that?"

"Sure. Like a plucked daisy."

"What're you up to in my kitchen?"

"The sink," Lucas said. "Been peelin' potatoes for dinner."

"That's not your job," Jean said.

"No more'n it's yours to ram around the range in that wagon."

"Couldn't you wait?"

"Long as you insist on doin' a man's work around here," Lucas said, "I reckon I can peel a few spuds. What's this?" He had noticed the bullet holes in the wagon. He shook his head like an angry bull as Woody told him how the holes got there. "I got a mind to ride over to Y Lightnin' and blow that hyena's head off."

"Easy, Lucas," Woody said. "You wouldn't stand a chance with McLouth."

"Time like this," Lucas said, "a man don't figure his chances." He started across the yard toward the corral.

"Dad, for heaven's sake," Jean said, "don't be so impulsive. There's no damage done, except to the wagon. Those holes can be plugged in a matter of minutes."

Lucas turned. He was still plenty mad, you could see that. His voice had a high, throaty sound to it. "Honey, it's no use tryin' to pretty the facts up. You been shot at. I guess Frank Gant figures he's such a big deal around here there's nothin' he can't get away with. You ask me, he's payin' off that excuse for a sheriff up at the county seat. Somebody's got to snub him short. It appears I'm elected. I'm goin' over and read the riot act to him."

"I'll go with you," Woody said in a voice that unconsciously mimicked Ruel Matheson's quiet manner.

Jean smiled gratefully at him. Her eyes misted.

"Both of you listen to me," she said. "If anything happened to—to either of you, I'd—I'd die."

A tear ran down her cheek. Lucas went to her and took her awkwardly into his arms, patting her on the back, comforting her as you'd comfort a baby.

"All right," he said at last, resignedly. "No need to take on."

Woody, with a long sigh of relief, led the two oxen across the yard and unhitched them from the wagon. Afterward, waiting for Jean's clang on the triangle that would call him to supper, he lay in his bunk, brooding over C Bar's situation and his own uncertain future.

Wish I had me one of those crystal balls about now, he couldn't help thinking.

Supper that night turned out to be Lucas's favorite meal of steak and pan-browned potatoes. This was Jean's way, Woody sensed, of smoothing down her father's ruffled pinfeathers. Lucas piled into his steak with gusto, but halfway through the meal he said, "What about this drifter that you say took McLouth's guns and brought him down the mountain? He goin' to get in any trouble on our account, honey?"

"I don't think so, Dad." Jean's slow smile, for some reason, gave Woody a jealous twinge. Lucas was watching him, he knew. He wondered if he had let his feelings show.

Lucas said to Jean idly, "What kind of a lookin' fella was he?"

"Who, Dad?"

"This young knight in shinin' armor that come to your rescue."

"I didn't say he was young. I didn't mention his age," Jean said.

"Well, what'd he look like?"

"Why—" For some reason, Woody noticed, Jean's cheeks were red. "I—I didn't notice. Not really. Let's see." She closed her eyes. "He was tall, and kind of knobby-jointed, but well put together. You know, strong, like Abe Lincoln. He had that kind of face too. Nice-looking in a homely way, if you know what I mean."

"Um," said her father. "Go on."

"He had sort of greenish-black eyes. One shoulder was a bit lower than the other, as if it might have been broken. His hair was black, and his skin had a coppery tint. It wouldn't surprise me to learn he's part Indian."

Her father pursed his lips over this information. "How old would you say he was, honey?"

"Not quite thirty. Why?"

"What was he wearin'?"

"Boots and Levis. A calico shirt under a black vest. What's this about, Dad? I don't see what you're trying to—"

Her father looked at her, a sly humor crinkling his eyes. "For somebody who says she wasn't payin' this fella no never-mind, you sure come up with the details."

Jean blushed. Woody sat there, feeling sweaty and uncomfortable, wondering why he should feel that way.

When later Lucas rode off toward town and his weekly get-together over a checkerboard with Yancey Jefford, Woody sat on the bunkhouse steps and whittled some pegs with which to plug the holes in the wagon.

Jean, when she'd finished the dishes, came across the yard and sat with him. Being alone with her like this, on the nights Lucas played checkers, never failed to quicken Woody's pulse.

To relieve a feeling of awkwardness, he said, "Doesn't seem to be anything Frank Gant'll stop at to get what he wants, does there?"

Jean's eyes came around curiously at him. She said after a moment, "Woody, if you're staying on here for my sake, I wish you wouldn't. It's not fair to let you risk your life for the wages Dad's able to pay."

"You sayin' I ought to've quit when the rest of the bunch did?"

"You had a perfect right to."

"I don't run out on an outfit in trouble," Woody said. In an abrupt change of the subject, he added, "What was Lucas tryin' to prove, askin' you all those questions about that drifter?"

"Dad likes to needle me," Jean said.

"You ask me, I was the one bein' needled."

"You?"

31

"What's the matter with me, anyway? Why don't he like me?"

"Why, he does." Jean patted Woody reassuringly on the arm. "Whatever gave you the idea he doesn't?"

"I dunno. I get a feelin' sometimes like he's laughin' up his sleeve at me."

"That's silly, Woody. Dad wouldn't laugh at you."

"Well, I suppose he appreciates me stayin' on. I work hard, and I'm steady. Maybe he's put me down for a plug horse. Good old dependable Woody."

"You *are* dependable," Jean said. "You're also a wonderful lovable person." As if to prove she meant what she said, she kissed him lightly on the mouth.

Her lips were warm, and soft as velvet. He felt like clapping an arm around her, giving her a kiss that would rock her. It was time she realized that good old Woody had another side to his nature. He stifled the impulse, afraid of releasing some devil within, of doing something for which Jean would never forgive him. He wondered miserably, as he let her draw away from him, if he was making a tactical error.

Jean stayed talking pleasantly, impersonally, another few minutes, then excused herself and returned to the house. Woody went in and lay on his bunk, staring dispiritedly out the window at a mass of dark clouds scudding across the sky.

Could rain tonight, he thought. It won't though. That's too much to hope for. Why didn't I grab her and give her a real kiss when she come pecking at me? What'm I scared of? What is it with Lucas? Why don't he like me? I s'pose it's no more'n natural for him to resent me. If I was him, and had a pip of a daughter like her, I wouldn't exactly cotton to the idea of some young buck shinin' up to her.

That thought eased Woody's mind. His eyes closed, and he slept.

He was awakened by a patter of rain on the roof. He lay in his bunk grinning, thinking what a good rain could do for C Bar. The rattle of a bit-chain, out in the yard, and a horse's soft snuffle, brought him out of his blankets and across the dark bunkhouse to the window.

Jean was outside in the yard, holding the reins of a

horse whose rider had slumped against the animal's neck. She held a lantern in her free hand, and glanced hopefully toward the bunkhouse. Woody fumbled into his clothes and hurried out to her.

"Who is it?"

"It's Ruel Matheson," Jean said. Woody thought curiously, Now how'd she manage to remember his name? He saw by the lantern's light that Matheson, who had been beaten badly, had uncoiled his rope before losing consciousness and tied himself in the saddle. He tipped his hat grudgingly to the man's courage.

"We'd better get him inside," Jean said. "He looks drenched through, and half frozen."

It took Woody some minutes to unravel the knots in Matheson's rain-soaked rope and to ease him down from the saddle. He carried the unconscious man toward the house.

"Where d' you want him?" he asked, staggering under his burden.

Jean led the way into her bedroom. Woody's feet dragged. He was frowning as he eased Matheson down. Somehow it didn't seem right to put the fellow in Jean's bed.

He helped her peel Matheson down to his flannels, which were more or less dry. Jean pulled the covers over him and laid a hand on his forehead. She looked up at Woody.

"Frank?"

"Who else?" Woody hesitated. "You sure you want him in your bed, all bloodied up the way he is?"

Jean was probing for the hurt man's pulse. "It's the only place for him. He's so terribly cold. He'll die, if he doesn't warm up soon ... You'd better ride to Chenango and fetch Doc Anders out here."

Woody stared out the window at the steady, slanting rain. "Tonight?"

Jean nodded, her eyes saying she had no choice but to ask this favor of him. Woody went out, sighing resignedly, and threw a saddle on his horse. He broke out his slicker, but long before he reached Chenango, water was trickling down inside his boots and under his collar.

33

He stopped off at the Jeffords' place to give Lucas the news. While Lucas went for the doctor, Woody dried out in front of a kitchen stove. Three cups of coffee put him in a pleasanter frame of mind, but by the time he'd got back out to C Bar with Lucas and the doctor, he was soaked through again, and his mood was sullen. He was silently cursing the drifter.

He saw as he entered Jean's room that she was in bed with the hurt man. He could feel his jaw sag. He stared at her in angry confusion as she rose from the bed, acting as though there were nothing the least bit unusual or untoward in her behavior.

Lucas's eyes seemed to say, "What's this, young lady?" but he was withholding judgment, Woody saw. Doc Anders regarded Jean with the unruffled composure of a man who has seen everything, is surprised at nothing.

He curled his fingers against the hurt man's wrist, and closed his eyes.

"How is he?" Jean asked.

The tired little man in the rumpled black suit laid his head against Ruel Matheson's chest. He unbuttoned the flannel undershirt and pursed his lips, breathing in sharply at sight of the bruised, battered ribcage. "You mean to tell me this man climbed on a horse, after taking a beating like this, and tied himself in the saddle?"

Jean nodded.

"Quite a man. Quite a man," said Doc Anders. He raised his eyebrows at Jean. "How'd you happen to be in bed with him?"

"It was the only way I could think of to get him warm," Jean said. "He was wet, and half frozen. I thought of heating some stones for bed warmers. But that would have taken too long. Getting in with him seemed to be the answer."

"Good girl." The doctor's quick, shrewd eyes looked toward Woody. "What's got your nose out of joint, son?"

"Nothin'."

"You don't approve of what she did, do you?"

"I never said—"

"Be proud of her," said the doctor. "She kept her head in a crisis. She did the best thing she could've done for this

34

fellow." Doc turned to Lucas. "You've got a fine girl here."

"I know," Lucas said.

Woody stood there, feeling foolish. Jean nodded down at the man in the bed. "Will he live, doctor?"

The apple-cheeked little man with the tolerant eyes wagged his head. "He hasn't a chance. Don't be blaming yourself, girl. You did everything anyone could've done for him."

"He's *got* to live," Jean said.

The urgency in her voice surprised Woody. Why has he got to? he thought. He was, almost at once, ashamed of himself. He looked at the unconscious man on the bed, and silently asked his forgiveness.

5

Some men are like cats, hard to kill. They enjoy, during their prime years, a kind of immortality, and live through experiences no ordinary man could survive.

Ruel Matheson, less than a week after his death was predicted, was able to sit up in bed. Four days later he moved out of the girl's room and across the C Bar's yard to the bunkhouse. He had, during that time, drifted into a relationship of easy familiarity with Lucas Wright and with the girl, who had delegated herself his nurse. For some reason he could not fathom he was on a less friendly footing with Woody Yarmon.

One night after dinner Lucas said, "You wouldn't by any chance be a checker player, would you, Ruel?"

Ruel regarded the older man gravely. "I play a little."

"Care for a game?" Lucas's manner was elaborately casual.

"Been a long time," Ruel said. "I'd be rusty."

"Well," Lucas said. "I won't say I don't keep in practice. I was playin' checkers in town, with a fellow named Yancey Jefford, the night you dragged in here."

"That so?"

"Yancey owns a little cowspread the other side of Chenango. Big, strappin' fella. Break you in half if he laid a hand on you. A couple years ago he married a woman who stands four-foot-eleven. Nowadays he has to keep a house in town, because Jenny won't live on a ranch. The Y J, he calls his outfit. In town it's spoke of as the 'Yes, Jenny'." Lucas grinned. "Don't it beat all the way a growed man'll let a woman curb-bit him?"

Ruel regarded the older man with a shrewd, amused speculation. It occurred to him he had been given more

36

detail on Yancey Jefford than was required. He's raisin' a smoke screen, he thought. Tryin' to soft-pedal the fact he rode all the way to town for a game of checkers.

"Let's see," Lucas said. "Where was we? You say it's been some time since you played? Why don't I spot you a couple of men, son? We'll see what happens."

"I don't know," Ruel said. "May not be able to make it interesting for you, even so."

"Let me worry about that." Lucas unfolded the board on the table, spilled the checkers onto it, and began separating reds from blacks with the quick, deft movements of a man who'd performed these rites often. "What color d' you prefer, son?"

Ruel shrugged, and now Jean, from where she sat across the room with Woody, said, "Are you sure you ought to play, Ruel? You're always so tired toward the end of the day."

"I'm up to one game of checkers," said Ruel, thanking her with his eyes for her concern.

"You don't know how seriously Dad takes the game."

"Honey, leave the man be. He ought to know if he feels up to this." Lucas glanced at Ruel. "All right, son?"

Ruel nodded. Lucas, having arranged the men on the board, removed the two men he'd promised to spot Ruel. He sat staring down at the board for a moment. His eyes came up speculatively toward Ruel's.

"You a betting man, are you?"

"I don't know," Ruel said. "It depends. What'd you have in mind?"

"Was wondering if you'd like to lay a little something on this, son."

"Dad," the girl said, "you stop. Just you stop. He's here as our guest. I won't have you—"

" 'Pears to me a grown man could decide a thing like that for himself," her father said drily. "What d' you say, son?"

Ruel pretended to give the matter considerable thought. He said, a shade of doubt in his voice, "How much of a little something did you have in mind?"

"What would you say to two dollars?"

Ruel stared down at the board, rubbing his chin. He

arched an eyebrow at Lucas. The older man said, "Well, then, let's say five dollars." Ruel still only sat there, a quizzical amusement in his eyes. Lucas stared at him, and said with the beginnings of caution, "What'd you have in mind?"

"Ten dollars has a nice substantial sound to it."

Lucas frowned. "You want to bet ten dollars on this?"

"I'll take a chance," Ruel said. "I feel lucky."

"Checkers ain't exactly a game of chance, son. There's skill involved."

"I feel lucky," Ruel said. To prove it, he took a ten dollar bill from his wallet and placed it beside the board on the table.

Lucas Wright grinned and reached for his wallet.

"Dad," the girl said, "you—"

"Keep out of this, honey." Lucas placed a crumpled bill atop Ruel's.

Ruel picked up the two men Lucas had spotted him, and replaced them on the board.

"What's the idea?" asked Lucas.

"You want first move?" Ruel asked.

Lucas sat there, staring at the men Ruel'd replaced on the board, at the pair of ten dollar bills on the table. "Go ahead," he said.

Ruel moved. The battle began, with Woody and the girl for kibitzers. Within five minutes Lucas was forced to jump two of Ruel's men, giving up three of his own in return. He had, until then, been humming softly. He stopped humming now, and studied the board with tight-mouthed concentration.

Even so, he soon fell into a one-for-two trap Ruel had set for him, and gave up another man. It was a matter of trading men off then. Lucas looked stunned as the last of his men was swept from the board. He stared at Ruel, who was finding it hard to maintain a poker face now.

The older man pushed himself back, away from the table, and clapped himself on the knees. "Hornswoggled," he said. "How d' you like this fella? He plays a *little*, he says. Not enough to make things interestin'."

"You asked for it, Dad." Jean turned to Ruel, smiling. "Dad plays at least once every week with Yancey Jefford.

Yancey's the second-best checker player in this part of the country."

Ruel was about to ask, "Who's the best?" Then he looked at Lucas's proudly rueful face, and saw there was no need of the question.

"Son," Lucas said, "where's a young fella like you learn to play checkers like that?"

"Here and there," Ruel said, tucking the two tens in his wallet.

"Wasn't intending to pry into your past, son."

"That's all right. I know you weren't."

Lucas regarded him, curious about him, trying not to show it. "Don't suppose you'd care for another game before we turn in?"

Ruel was tempted. Lucas was clearly out to get even. The girl, for her part, seemed pleased that her father'd found somebody to give him a run for his money. Woody Yarmon had that strained look of a man trying to put a good face on a situation he didn't much care for. Time I got out of here, Ruel thought.

"Maybe tomorrow night, Lucas," He went out and across the yard to the bunkhouse.

He slept soundly that night, and woke up feeling strong enough to try his luck on horseback.

"You two riding out today?" he asked Lucas and Woody at breakfast.

"Why?" asked Lucas.

"I'll ride along, if you can stand company," Ruel said.

"Are you up to it?"

"One sure way to find out," Ruel grinned.

They rode out within the half hour. Lucas and Woody, in deference to Ruel's condition, held their horses down to a canter. At the outset Ruel had some bad moments, but after a mile or so of that rocking-chair gait he felt stronger, and more alive, than he'd felt in days.

There was no need for him to stay on at C Bar. He could leave any time, he thought, and was surprised how little pleasure he took in the prospect.

They passed one dried-up water hole after another, and halted finally alongside the dry bed of Whitewoman Creek, which had been Lucas's principal source of water until Frank Gant dammed it.

"You see how I'm fixed?" Lucas said. "That rain two weeks ago kept my critters alive, but I can't hold on here without crick water. Frank Gant's betting on it. He's posted a guard at the dam, with orders to shoot anyone who tries tamperin' with it."

"Would the law stand for that?" Ruel frowned.

"The law's a hundred miles off, in the county seat." Lucas made a wry face. "Our excuse for a sheriff spends more time sittin' on the courthouse steps, makin' himself agreeable to the votin' public, than he spends in his office. He ain't interested in what goes on down here."

"I understand there's a marshal in Chenango."

"And there's where he stays. In Chenango."

"What about your ranching neighbors?"

"That'd be Yancey," Lucas said. "His wife ain't about to let him throw in with me against Frank. There's just him and me. Frank could grind the pair of us to a pulp, if he chose to. I dunno what to do, son."

Ruel turned toward Woody Yarmon. "You grew up hereabouts, Woody," he said. "How soon do you look for rain?"

Woody rubbed his neck, considering in his slow, sober way. "Gettin' on toward the tag end of summer. I look for a drought breaker any day now. But it'll take more'n that to save our bacon."

Ruel stared down along the dry creek bed. He was silent so long that Lucas glanced curiously at him. "You got something in mind, son?"

Ruel pointed at the far bank, which had been deeply cut by flood water some time in the past. "I see you have a clay subsoil. I worked for an outfit down in the Nations that had a subsoil like that."

"Oh?" Lucas said.

"They had no cricks or wells or water holes down there. But their critters never went thirsty."

"How'd they manage?" Lucas asked.

"You've heard of a dug tank?"

Lucas shook his head. "Until two years ago I kept a

40

country store, son. I'm a greenhorn in this cattle-raising business . . . . Woody, what's he mean by a dug tank?"

Woody lifted his shoulders and let them fall.

Ruel said, "You scoop out a hole in the ground, in the shape of a saucer, and line its sides and bottom with clay."

"You mean a crude affair like that'd hold water?"

"If you tamp the clay down tight it will," Ruel said.

"You think that's the answer for us, son?"

"It could make all the difference," Ruel said, "if it rains."

"Hell and damnation," Lucas said. "What're we waitin' for? Let's put in some dug tanks."

Ruel couldn't help grinning at the older man's enthusiasm.

Woody Yarmon said in his sober way, "Suppose it don't rain?"

"Life is a gamble," said Ruel.

Lucas's head bobbed in agreement. He turned in the saddle and spoke to Woody. "Better turn in early tonight."

"What for?"

"Come mornin'," Lucas said, "you and I'll be takin' turns with a pick and shovel."

Woody's eyes narrowed, as if to say that was no work for a self-respecting cowpuncher. Ruel felt sympathy for him.

Lucas said, "Ruel, I'm hopin' you'll boss this job, till we get the hang of it."

Ruel, glancing at Woody, saw a murky resentment in the stocky cowpuncher's eyes. "You don't need my help on this, Lucas."

"I'd appreciate it if you'd stand by at the start, son."

Ruel had a feeling of walls closing in on him. In some way the checker game last night had brought him closer to Lucas.

"I might choose the locations," he said.

He chose one within the hour, on the way back to Lucas's buildings. In the morning he rode out alone in search of additional locations, while Lucas and Woody fell to with pick and shovels. Ruel had a feeling, as he trotted along, of being kept under surveillance. He had spent part of his life on the dodge, and had learned not to shrug off such warnings. He whipped around in the saddle and raked the horizon with a sweeping glance. He could see no movement, no telltale dust puff to betray a trailer's position.

He told himself he was imagining things, but could not convince himself of it. Before he'd finished his morning's work he was as tensed up inside as a treed bobcat.

Lucas and Woody completed one tank that day, and scooped out the hole for a second. In the morning Lucas had to drag himself out of bed. Although his aging, storekeeper's hands, unused to plying a shovel, had puffed out in the joints and stiffened during the night, he stayed on the job, taking his regular turn on the shovel with Woody.

When the older man became dangerously red in the face, Ruel insisted on taking a turn. In two minutes he was forced to set the shovel aside and rest in the shade of a tree.

He was no more help the next day. He chafed in the role of spectator while Lucas and Woody, working like slaves, completed a third and forth installation.

Woody almost shook the bunkhouse down with his snoring that night. Ruel, after trying for some time to ignore the racket, carried his blankets out behind the bunkhouse, and lay on the grass under the stars.

There were only a few innocent-looking clouds in the sky as he fell asleep. But there is no predicting the weather in high country. He had proof of that toward morning, when a ʼraindrop, splattering against his forehead, woke him.

He snatched his bedding up and carried it into the bunkhouse, grinning. He probably ought to awaken Woody and tell him about the rain. He couldn't bring himself to disturb the snoring cowpuncher. He wouldn't thank me for it, Ruel thought. He never liked the cut of my jib to begin with.

He moved along the aisle between the bunks, finding his way as easily as a cat, and reached the door in time to see the girl step out onto the gallery of the ranch house and fling her arms wide.

Crazy thing to do, he thought. She'll be drenched. He

knew how she felt though. She hugged herself, rocking slowly, and Ruel thought, I ought to go over there. Times like this are better shared with somebody.

At the thought of being with the girl in the dead of the night he felt his heart pound. Easy now, he thought. Don't get any ideas. That girl's not for you.

She went back into the house. Ruel sought his bunk and lay staring up at the shadow-patterned ceiling, telling himself to get the girl out of his mind. An hour later he was still thinking of her.

He slept, finally, and woke up to find Woody Yarmon peering out the bunkhouse window in the gray light of dawn. The rain had slacked off now, Ruel saw.

"You see this?" Woody asked.

Ruel nodded. "I was awake when it started."

"You could've let a man know," Woody said.

"I could. I didn't have the heart to wake you up, the way you were goin' at it," Ruel said.

"Thanks," Woody said, in a friendlier tone. He looked embarrassed. "This is the second rain we've had since you came to C Bar. Seems like you're lucky for us."

"A man makes his luck," Ruel shrugged.

Woody watched a rivulet of water run down the window glass. "You made some for us when you suggested puttin' those tanks in."

"You and Lucas did the work, Woody."

Woody shifted his weight from one leg to the other, and cleared his throat. "I been actin' kind of stand-offish with you," he said. "I hope you'll believe me when I say I regret it."

He smiled, and put out his hand. Ruel, as he took the man's hand and shook it, had a tight, dry feeling in the throat, and he could feel his eyes misting.

There was a lot of conjecture, at breakfast, as to how much rain had fallen, and how those dug tanks were holding. Jean rode along out with them to see.

Lucas, as they cantered along, asked Woody how many of Jean's wheatcakes he'd eaten.

"I don't know," Woody said. "I suppose six or seven."

"Hell," Lucas said, with a sly wink at Ruel, "if you'd stacked them any higher you could get a job in the circus.

43

A good balancin' act is always in demand. You sure put one on with them wheatcakes this mornin'."

Woody grinned, to show he could take a ribbing. Again Lucas winked at Ruel, including him in this fun, and Ruel wondered how it would be to ride for one brand, year in and year out, until you became like one of the family.

They idled along through rolling, sage-dappled hills. The air, washed clean by the rain, had a pungent, wet-hay smell to it. As they passed a prairie dog town the little creatures, not afraid of them, sat on the edges of the terraced mounds surrounding their burrows, jerking their tails and squeaking.

Ruel and the girl exchanged smiles, and Woody, noticing, frowned.

They topped a rise. Below them in a wide shallow swale lay the first of the dug tanks Lucas and Woody had put in.

Ruel had expected to find it full of rain water. There was no water in the installation. It had the appearance of a mudhole through which a herd of cattle had been driven.

Lucas Wright's eyes, as he turned to Ruel, were bitter.

"What do you make of this?" he asked.

6

Ruel, as he rode down into the swale, was remembering the feeling he'd had of being followed while he scouted out these locations. A half-dozen scrawny-looking steers clustered about what was left of the tank, poking their noses into the muck. One animal lifted its head and bawled. Ruel felt somehow guilty, as though he were responsible for the brute's frustration.

He studied the hoofprints in and around the installation.

"Three men," he said. "They must've milled their horses around in there for ten minutes, to churn things up like that. It's too bad. Be dry as a bone here an hour from now." He pointed eastward. "They were on their way to our next tank when they left here."

Lucas gave a bulllike shake of his head. "When d' you reckon that was?"

"Half an hour ago."

Lucas turned toward his daughter. "Honey, you mosey on home."

"Why?" Jean asked.

"You go along."

"What are you going to do, Dad?"

"Protect what's mine." Lucas's glance sought out Ruel's. "Ride in with her. This ain't your party."

Ruel stared at the mountain northward, at the high, buff-colored ridges with patches of aspen near their flinty crests. He pulled his horse half around, then halted the dun with knee pressure.

"I'll stay."

"No reason you should."

"I'll stay." Ruel could feel the girl watching him, feel her interest in him now.

"I'm staying too, Dad."

Lucas looked at her with mingled pride and misgiving. He sighed. "Let's get goin' then," he said.

A child could have followed the deeply indented hoofprints that led away from the installation. With Ruel in the lead, they crossed a series of low, moundlike hills. Ruel reined in finally, staring down a long tilt of land at their second installation.

Frank Gant, Harry McLouth, and a tall, slope-shouldered red-haired man were pulling their horses around through the water, laughing and splashing.

Lucas's jaw set. Something wild—unstable—brightened the older man's eyes. Ruel, in a deliberately casual voice, asked, "Who's the man on the bay?"

"Red Coombs. Frank Gant's foreman." Lucas spurred his horse down the grade.

Ruel followed, pulling Woody and the girl along with him.

Frank Gant saw them coming. His head turned and he spoke to McLouth. The gunman sent his horse scrambling out of the muck onto level ground. He loosened his gun in its flapless holster.

McLouth was wearing the black sombrero he'd worn that first day, Ruel saw; he recognized the hat by the brim which had been slit and threaded with rawhide. He couldn't see the hole his bullet had made through the crown. McLouth must have patched it.

Lucas had reined in, facing Frank.

"Mister," he said, in the twangy voice of a man near his boiling point, "what d' you think you're doin'?"

"I guess it's plain enough. . . . I wouldn't, if I were you," Frank said, as Lucas dropped his hand toward his gun.

Lucas sat there, glaring at the big man, who seemed to have himself well under control.

"McLouth don't like seein' me threatened, Lucas," he said.

"Don't he?"

Frank shook his head. "I'm tellin' you this to be fair."

"Dad," Jean said, "don't—"

"I'll handle this," Lucas said.

"Frank said. "You thought about my offer for C Bar?"

"I've thought about it."

"Well?"

"You can go to hell with that offer."

Frank's eyes thinned. The corners of his mouth tightened. "I'd go easy on that kind of talk, if I was—"

"Get off my land, Frank."

McLouth, Ruel saw, was watching Frank, awaiting orders, his pale eyes glittering with impatience. Lucas grinned at the gunman, as if to say, "You don't scare me." Ruel could see how Lucas's attitude galled Frank.

The big man inclined his head toward the dug tank and said to McLouth, "You sure that job's finished?"

McLouth gave him a blank look. His lips pulled away from his teeth. He turned his horse back toward the water. Ruel saw the storm warnings in Lucas's eyes, saw the girl bite down on her lower lip.

"McLouth?" he said, dealing himself in now, and the gunman drew rein.

"Somethin' on your mind?" he asked, leaning back in the saddle.

"Keep away from that water." Ruel hooked his thumb in his shellbelt. His eyes never left those of the professional killer, who brought his horse slowly around.

Lucas spoke out of the side of his mouth. "Better not crowd this sidewinder too close, son."

McLouth's smile, Ruel sensed, was the mask some men put on as a prelude to killing. He drew in a long breath and exhaled, thinking, I'm not a well man. I'm still weak as bar whisky, and, damn him, he knows it.

There was a humming in his ears. He had a feeling of weightlessness. It was as though he were in suspension, somewhere between dreaming and waking. He heard Frank Gant say, "Let it ride, Harry," and wondered if his ears were playing tricks on him.

"What for?" McLouth said. "I know what I'm doin'."

"I said let it ride." Frank might have been speaking to an aroused, surly dog.

McLouth shrugged, and stared sullenly at Ruel.

Frank spoke to Lucas. "Matheson working for you now?"

"What's it to you?" Lucas asked.

47

Frank's eyes had that nettled expression of a man just barely managing to hold his temper. He said, "Why don't you take what I've offered you for your place, Lucas? One way or another, I'm goin' to have it."

"You been told to git," Lucas said.

Frank scowled. His eyes sought the girl's, asking for her help now.

"Git!" Lucas said.

"I'm through foolin' with you," Frank said. "Don't buy any more supplies in Chenango."

"Why not?"

"You'll never get out of town with them."

"Won't I?" said Lucas. "Why won't I?"

"I'll see to it."

Lucas's jaw sagged. "You're not God Almighty. You can't keep a man from buyin' what he needs."

Frank smiled coldly at Lucas and apologetically at the girl, who gave him back a stony stare. Frank pulled his horse around and rode off, taking McLouth and the strangely taciturn red-haired man with him.

Frank Gant turned his head for a covert glance at McLouth, who had been silent now for ten minutes. The gunman, as he rode, stared at a white marking between his horse's ears, sulking, Frank guessed, because he'd been refused permission to gun Ruel Matheson down.

"You should've let me have him," McLouth said, as if reading Frank's thoughts.

"You may be lucky I didn't."

"Lucky?" McLouth said. "How?"

"He didn't look a damn bit scared of you."

"Fools don't know enough to be scared when they ought to."

Frank smiled, and the gunman, seeing it, added, "Maybe you don't think he had reason to be scared."

"Take it easy," Frank said. "You're too touchy."

But McLouth's pride had been pricked. He fell into a long brooding silence. Later, as they idled along a dug road bordered by pine trees, the gunman reined in. He pointed at one of the trees from which a lower limb had been broken.

48

"See that knothole?"

"I see it," Frank said. "What about it?"

McLouth climbed down. He took a silver dollar out of his pocket, and loosened his gun in the holster. Holding his gun hand out, palm downward, he placed the coin atop it.

"That tree," he said, "is Matheson. We'll call that knothole his heart."

As he spoke, his hand whipped down and up. His gun was in it. Flame burst from the muzzle. Before the coin reached the ground, his slug gouged a hole in the tree, less than an inch from his target.

McLouth turned toward Frank, pleased with himself, a dog expecting a pat on the head and a word of praise. Frank gave him the deadpan expression he had cultivated years ago as an itinerant gambler.

"You missed."

"Just," McLouth said.

"A miss is a miss, Harry," Frank said. He indicated the bullet hole in the tree. "From what I've seen of Matheson, I'm not sure that's good enough."

McLouth's face was getting red. "Listen—"

"Some men fight on like animals after they're hurt," Frank said. "Matheson's that kind. Take a slug in the chest and cut you down while he's falling."

McLouth pointed at the hole in the tree. "I ain't apologizin' for that kind of shootin'. You know anyone can do any better? If that ain't good enough for you—"

"Take it easy," Frank said.

"You take it easy," McLouth said.

"What're you getting sore for?"

"I ain't sore. I'm tellin' you, is all. You know anybody who can do what I just done?" McLouth turned toward Red Coombs. "Give it a try, Red. See how close you can come."

Frank's foreman shook his head. "I'm no fast-draw artist. I never claimed to be anything special in that line."

McLouth, Frank saw, was unable to hide his disappointment.

"Give it a try, Red," Frank said. "It won't kill you."

Red shrugged. He climbed down off his horse. He placed the silver dollar on the back of his hand, as he'd seen McLouth do. After a moment's wait to achieve concentration, he dropped his hand toward his gun.

There was no rhythm, no grace, Frank saw, to Red's motion. He was slow in easing the hammer back, slow in lifting the weapon. Although the coin struck the ground before he got his shot off, he missed the target, pulling to the right of the knothole. His slug stripped bark from the tree, and came within a hair's breadth of missing it altogether.

Frank regarded the redheaded man. "You better practice with that thing."

"I'm no gunfighter. I never claimed to be one, Frank."

"That's not the point." Frank's eyes came up. "If a man can't use his gun any better'n that, he's a fool to wear it."

Red glanced at McLouth with resentment, then indicated Frank's gun, his eyes asking, "What about you?"

Frank said, "It's a little different with me, Red. I've got a lot of gunhandy men workin' for me."

Red Coombs picked the silver dollar up and gave it back to McLouth, who was grinning now, Frank saw. The three of them rode on, their horses kicking up dust from the road.

Remembering how Matheson had thrown the gauntlet down to McLouth, Frank thought, He'd've drawn on Harry if I hadn't taken a hand in the proceedings. He looks kind of peaked, but he sure as hell doesn't scare. He must be fast—but how fast?

The question nagged at him as he rode along. He drew rein finally. Harry McLouth and Red Coombs pulled up alongside and glanced curiously, expectantly at him.

"Ride on in, boys," Frank told them.

"Where you goin'?" McLouth asked.

Frank gave the gunman a look, ignoring the question. "See you at the ranch," he said.

He turned and rode back, at a leisurely pace, to where McLouth had staged his gunslinging exhibition. Frank climbed down, took a shiny fifty-cent piece from his pocket, placed it on his wrist, stared at the knothole briefly, and brought his hand down.

The coin had dropped to within an inch of the ground when he triggered. His slug lodged in the edge of the knothole. With the acrid, not unpleasant odor of burnt gunpowder crinkling his nose, he pushed the empty casing out of his gun and inserted a live cartridge. He was grinning, whistling through his teeth softly.

Years ago, before he'd tried his hand at gambling for his livelihood, he had paid a gunman to teach him to shoot. He had, after six months of almost unceasing practice, become more adept than his tutor. Later, he had killed two men over card tables.

Frank regarded his ability to draw and shoot as insurance. He made a point, now and then, of riding up into the hills and shooting off a few rounds, keeping his hand in. He never talked about these excursions. A man's gun speed, as he saw it, was an ace card up his sleeve. The men Frank unfortunately had had to kill had gone down with astonishment in their eyes.

Frank gave the wooden handle of his gun a complacent, approving pat now as he let it fall back into the holster. Maybe, before the dust settled on this quarrel with C Bar, Ruel Matheson would fall with that same astonished look on his face.

7

After supper, which was necessarily late, Ruel perched on the bunkhouse steps and tried not to think about Jean. You'd have thought McLouth would be uppermost in his mind. He'd nearly traded shots with the fellow. All he could think about was the glance the girl'd given him during the meal. He had a hunch she wanted a private word with him, that she had something to tell him.

It was darker now. A sliver of moon peered out from behind a cloud, bathing the house and the ranch yard with shadowy light. Out on the grass flat a cicada chirped, and was answered. Ruel built himself a cigarette and had smoked it halfway down when the girl came out of the house and stood stretching her arms, luxuriating, Ruel guessed, in the fact that her dishes were done and her day's work finished.

She crossed the yard toward him. She had what looked like a paper bag in her hand. As she neared him, she dropped it, and stood peering down, unable to find it in the dark.

Ruel went over and picked it up for her.

"What's in it?" he asked, as he handed it to her.

"Woody brought some chocolates from town, Ruel. I thought you might like one."

Ruel had no sweet tooth. He took one anyway, grinning as he munched on it. "I'm not sure Woody had me in mind when he bought these."

Jean's low laugh had a pleasant, friendly sound. "He wouldn't begrudge you one piece, Ruel." She went on wonderingly, "However did you manage to see them on the ground?"

"Mother nature blessed me with cat eyes."

52

They sat side by side on the top step. The girl caught up one rounded knee between her clasped hands and leaned back. A faint, clean fragrance floated about her. Ruel wanted, for no reason that made any sense to him, to reach out and put his hand on her hair.

"What're Woody and your Dad doin'?"

"They're trying to decide what to do."

"You mean—about our friend Gant?"

He saw her nod in response to his question. "Ruel, I—I want to thank you for what you've done."

"I haven't done anything."

"But you have. Whose idea was it to put in those dug tanks? And what do you suppose would have happened today, if you hadn't come between Dad and that killer?"

She put her hand on his, and it surprised him to learn that this girl was made of warm flesh and blood like himself. He had been cut off, during a great part of his life, from normal contact with women. He tended to idealize them.

He curled an arm around Jean's shoulders. With his other arm, he pulled her toward him. He crushed his mouth against hers. For an instant, he could have sworn she gave herself to his embrace. He knew the softness, the sweetness, of her parted lips. She murmured protestingly, "Please, Ruel," and turned her head away.

He held her more tightly, reminding himself that she'd responded to his kiss for an instant. He cupped her chin in his hand, and forced another kiss on her as she tried to pull away.

There was no pleasure in this, he found after a moment. He let her go.

"Why didn't you stop when I asked you to, Ruel?"

He sat there wondering what he could say, thinking, She's decent. I been treating a decent girl like some little chippy.

"Sorry. It won't happen again," he said, a dryness in his throat, an ache in his chest now.

Their voices must have carried across the yard. Lucas and Woody had come out onto the gallery of the house.

"Jean?" Lucas called.

"Yes, Dad." She was smoothing her dress, touching her

53

hair into place as she stepped out of the shadow there in front of the bunkhouse.

"You all right?"

Ruel felt something tense up within him as he waited for the girl's reply to her father.

"Of course, I'm with Ruel. I'll be in in a minute."

Lucas, satisfied, turned back into the house. Woody, Ruel noticed, lingered a suspicious instant before following Lucas.

"I'd better go in, Ruel," Jean said.

Ruel watched her move away from him across the moon-shadowed yard, feeling strangely let down. He went in and lay on his bunk, remembering how she had felt in his arms. He touched his lip with his tongue, savoring the aftertaste of her kiss. Quit this, he thought. That girl's not for you.

When Woody came across from the house, Ruel was still lying there in the dark, puffing on his third cigarette in a half hour. Woody struck a match to the candle mounted in a sardine can on the crude, homemade table.

"What was all that between you and Jean?" he asked.

"All that?"

"I'm askin' you what happened out on the steps there."

"What does she say happened out there?"

"Nothing."

"That's it then." Ruel glanced up. "You wouldn't doubt the lady's word, would you?"

"She looked kind of flustered when she came in the house. By God, mister, if you been gettin' out of line—"

"Look," said Ruel, "why don't you take the load off your feet and relax. You're all steamed up. And there's no reason for it."

Woody stood there, his big hands balled into fists, his chest heaving as he regarded Ruel. "You say nothin' happened?"

"Nothing for you to worry about."

"What's that mean?"

"Whatever you want it to mean," Ruel'd had a bellyful of this, and he let the other man know it, glaring at him as he rose to face him.

Woody, instead of backing off, blurted out at him, "Who *are* you mister?"

"The name's Matheson."

"That ain't what I mean."

"What *do* you mean?"

"You been at C Bar two weeks, and what do we know about you? Nothin'."

"So?" Ruel said, lifting his eyebrows.

"Jean's decent. I'm goin' to marry her, if she'll have me." Woody hesitated, then plunged. "And right now I'm buildin' a fence around her where any man who refuses to talk about his past is concerned."

Ruel could feel his face tighten. I ought to pop you one, buster, he thought. But he could see the other man's side of this. Woody was only trying to protect Jean. And he's right. I've got no business mooning after that girl, not with my background.

"Let's get some shuteye," he said, crawling back into his bunk. Woody stood scowling down at him, then he sat on the edge of his bunk and began to unbutton his shirt. In a matter of minutes he had turned in and was snoring, as though nothing had happened.

Ruel envied him his ability to slough things off. In the morning, he supposed, the stocky man in his single-minded serious way would pick up the discussion where they'd left off. Ruel found no pleasure at all in that prospect. After tossing and turning for several hours he fished his boots out from under his bunk and, carrying them and his clothes, tiptoed out of the long, low frame building. He dressed outside in the dark.

Within fifteen minutes he had caught up and saddled his dun horse, Tony, and was leading the animal out C Bar's lane at a walk. When he was beyond earshot of the buildings, he climbed into the saddle.

The night was clammily cold, and his mood was bleak. He had seen the last of Jean Wright, he knew.

Why did I kiss her? What made me think I had to force a kiss on her? I *did*n't have to, at first. She let me. Cut it out, he thought. That girl's turnin' your insides to jelly.

He was reminded of his past. He didn't often allow himself to think back. There were few things in his past life that he cared to dwell on. He had spent a great deal of time in prison. He remembered, now, something a cellmate had told him: "We'll never get the stink of jail off us, Ruel. You're branded different when you've done time. Wait'll you get out, you'll see. There's an invisible wall between a man who's been in jail and one who hasn't. And nobody gets past it."

It was true, Ruel thought. He had never felt he belonged at C Bar, not really. Time I was getting away from there. And from that girl.

He had the familiar emptiness inside, like a kind of hunger that had nothing to do with food, as he thought of the girl.

The sun began to gray in the sky eastward. Dawn would come coldly, he sensed, and he shivered. For the first time now he looked at what he was doing through the girl's eyes. He kneed the dun to a halt, and scowled down at the animal's short-cropped mane. After a bitter debate with himself, he headed back the way he had come.

He saw no sign of Lucas or Woody, when he dragged into C Bar around eight in the morning. Jean came out of the house, wiping her forehead with the back of her arm, shading her eyes as she looked at him.

"Climb down, Ruel," she said pleasantly. "Did you forget something?"

Ruel fumbled his hat off as he dismounted. "Only my manners."

"Your manners?"

"I don't know what got into me last night. I'm here to tell you again I'm sorry about that. And to say a proper goodbye."

Jean stared at him, an unaccustomed gravity in her blue eyes.

"How far did you get before you turned around?" she asked.

Ruel pointed southwestward, toward a series of low, stony ridges. "Halfway up into those hills."

"And you rode all the way back to say what you just said?"

He nodded. "I was hopin' to say it in front of your father and Woody. I don't want to be the cause of any misunderstandin' around here." He made himself look her in the eye. "I been doin' a lot of thinkin' about the way I acted last night."

"Don't blame yourself too much. Everybody is tempted that way, Ruel."

"Everybody doesn't act on temptation."

"You were tempted to ride out in the night, too. I notice you're back. You seem to wind up doing what's right when you've had time to think, Ruel."

He thanked her with his eyes, thinking that Woody Yarmon had better hurry up and toss a loop on this girl.

"You're a better man than you give yourself credit for being, Ruel. Don't look at me that way. It's true."

He could feel warmth in his cheeks. He started to put his hat on, then thrust it behind him.

Jean smiled. "All right. I won't mention it again if you'll come inside and eat something. You look famished."

Later, when he'd had breakfast, and was again ready to ride, he said, "Where'll I find Woody and your father?"

"Why?"

"May's well do things right while I'm at it. Thought I'd say goodbye to them."

"Really, you needn't. I could say it for you." Jean's eyes skittered away, unwilling to meet Ruel's. That's odd, he thought. That's not like her.

"Aren't they out on the range?"

As she hesitated, Ruel's eyes shifted toward the horse pasture. Her father's buckskin was down in there, grazing, with Woody's bay for company. Ruel crossed the yard and studied the ground in front of the barn. He saw a pattern of wheel marks and hoofprints which indicated that the ranch wagon had been pulled out of the shed, and the mare hooked up to it, some time this morning.

He turned to Jean, frowning. "Where'd they go? Into Chenango?"

Still she hesitated, as if she hated to speak. For the first time now, Ruel saw the concern in her eyes.

"I should've known," he said. "Your dad couldn't wait to throw Frank's ultimatum in his face, could he?"

"Dad's never let anybody order him around."

"How long ago did they leave?"

"An hour before you came. I didn't want you to know. You've had enough trouble on our account. Since you *do* know, may I ask one last favor?"

"Name it."

"Go after them, Ruel. Talk some sense into Dad. There's no telling what will happen when he reaches town. He has such a temper, and—Ruel, I'm worried. Woody and I both tried to stop Dad. He wouldn't listen."

"What makes you think he'd listen to me?"

"Dad's impressed with you, Ruel. You—beat him at checkers."

Ruel grinned at the reasoning. But she was serious, he saw.

"I'll go," he said.

She squeezed his arm, her eyes thanking him, and he stepped back, not trusting himself so close to this bewitching creature.

"I better make tracks," he said, "if I'm to catch them before they reach town."

He climbed aboard the dun and rode out. At the end of the lane he looked back, and saw Jean standing in front of the house where he had left her. She waved, he waved back. She is not too put out about what happened last night, he thought strangely.

As he loped along he asked himself how it would be to be married to a girl like Jean. Her and me, he thought, in a little place of our own. Neighbors close enough to be handy without getting underfoot. And maybe a couple of kids.

Good-looking kids, with Jean for their mother. They wouldn't show Injun as much as I do. They might not show it at all. And they'd be raised right. They wouldn't have the kind of upbringin' I had. They'd go to school regular, and she'd teach 'em manners. They'd be fine, happy youngsters and they'd grow up to be real human beings. Just because the old man messed me up don't mean my kids'd have to be messed up.

My kids—that's a laugh. She'd never marry me, not if she knew what I've been and done. No more'n I'd dare to ask her. Wouldn't it be somethin' though, if she'd have me. God!

Why's it mean so much to me? Lots of men have lived single, and some of them seem to enjoy it. Maybe it's because I never had any family, not really. What you don't have is what you want in this life.

Quit it, he thought. I go runnin' on like this, and I'll start feelin' sorry for myself.

He rode with more purpose. After an hour he dropped down off a limestone bluff into a shallow valley through which a stream meandered. He rode along a barbwire fence clogged with tumbleweed. Rounding a craggy upthrust which seemed out of place here in the valley, he overtook Lucas and Woody in C Bar's spring wagon.

Lucas reined in. Both men turned on the wagon seat to regard Ruel:

"Howdy?" Lucas said. "Where in hell'd you vamoose to last night, son?"

8

Where he'd been, Ruel thought, wasn't important. He indicated the wagon. "You sure this is wise, Lucas?"

"I'm goin' in."

"You think Frank Gant was bluffing?"

Lucas shrugged.

"He wasn't bluffing," Ruel said with conviction.

"I'm still goin' in."

Ruel glanced at Woody. The stocky cowpuncher gave a weary shake of his head, as if to say that when Lucas was in this mood it was no use talking to him.

"I'll ride in with you," said Ruel.

"I can't accept any more help from you, son."

"You think Frank's playing games with you?" Ruel frowned.

"If it's all the same to you, son, I'd as soon not discuss it."

Lucas had that look of a troubled man anxious to put trouble behind him. He flicked his reins, murmuring, "Thanks, anyway, son." Ruel watched the wagon rattle along the rutted dirt road.

Lucas, Ruel thought, you're goin' to get killed. Is that what you want? You think that's what *she'd* want?

One last favor, he thought, and he saw now that he had let the girl down. He could circle the town and come in from the far side, make himself handy, at least, in case he was needed. Lucas won't like it, he thought. But it's a free country.

He pulled off the road, knifing up into the hills, and rode due west for some miles. He came down into the town out of an evergreen forest, with pine scent in his

60

nostrils, and racked his horse under a mangy, lightning-gashed cottonwood outside the Cattlemen's Hotel.

He settled into a rocking chair on the hotel porch and made himself a cigarette. Three horses wearing Y Lightning's brand stood outside the Straight Shot saloon down the street. Ruel watched them stamp their feet in the dust and switch at flies.

One animal, smarter or, perhaps, more susceptible to heat than its companions, kept thrusting its head down under the tierail into the shade afforded by the saloon's corrugated-tin awning.

Ruel was still there on the hotel porch when Woody and Lucas came rattling around the bank corner in C Bar's wagon. As they came abreast of him, he deserted his rocking chair and draped a leg along the porch railing.

"What're you doin' here?" Lucas challenged.

"Figured I'd have a look at Chenango," Ruel said, "before I left this country. No harm in that, is there?"

Lucas didn't reply. Three men, as Ruel spoke, had emerged from the saloon down the street. They stood under its awning, staring up toward the hotel. McLouth, in the middle, wore his habitual faint scowl. His companions, strangers to Ruel, were smiling as though they felt smiles were required of them.

Ruel heard a footfall behind him. He turned, watching a tall, gray-haired man step out onto the hotel porch from the lobby. A badge worn down inside the man's vest pocket, partially hidden from view, caught Ruel's eye. The law, he thought. That's timely.

The gray-haired man eyed Lucas and Woody. His glance moved along the street toward the Y Lightning trio.

"What's goin' on?" he said to Lucas.

"Nothin'."

"Don't tell me."

"Con," Lucas said, nodding toward Ruel, "this here's Ruel Matheson. Ruel, say howdy to Marshal Con Wishard."

Con Wishard acknowledged Ruel's murmured, "Howdy?" with a dry nod. He said again to Lucas, "What's goin' on?"

"Nothin'."

The marshal turned for a questioning glance at Woody. This man's hard, steady eyes, Ruel thought, could bore a hole in sheet metal.

"What about this, Yarmon?"

"Woody turned uneasily toward Lucas. "Tell him, why don't you?"

"Tell me what?" asked the marshal, and now Woody, avoiding Lucas's glance, brought the lawman up-to-date on the situation. Wishard scowled as he listened. He was silent a moment, then he said, "Wait here," and stepped down off the hotel porch.

"Con," Lucas said, "where you goin'?"

"Frank Gant doesn't own this town, Lucas. I'll tell you what you can and can't do in Chenango."

Wishard moved out into the street, a tall, slender, aging man who carried himself with military erectness. He walked down toward the Straight Shot, toward Y Lightning's hard-case trio. His stride never faltered as he moved steadily forward.

McLouth's scowl gave way to a cocky, self-conscious smile as the lawman approached him. Wishard halted twenty yards short of the trio, and said something to McLouth that Ruel could not hear.

McLouth spoke in reply. Wishard tensed, as at an insult. He jerked an arm at McLouth and his hard-bitten companions. Ordering them out of town, Ruel thought.

McLouth shook his head, waved his partners aside, and planted himself in the street, facing the marshal. Ruel knew then what was coming. He had a sinking feeling inside.

McLouth smiled and spat, as if in contempt of the aging lawman. Con Wishard went for his gun then, but he never got it out of the holster. As he was lifting the weapon, McLouth, who had drawn with wicked speed, shot him through the forearm.

The marshal's gun fell back into the scabbard. He supported his injured arm with his good arm and stared at McLouth in impotent anger. Lifting his head, walking with pride, he moved on down the street, turning off presently into an alleyway between buildings.

McLouth regarded Lucas and Woody, a challenge in his eyes. Woody, Ruel saw, had lost some of his ruddy color. Lucas said to him, "Make yourself scarce. I can stomp my own snakes."

"I'm stayin'," Woody said. Good man, thought Ruel, who had watched the play of emotion on Woody's face as he struggled toward that decision.

"How d' you want to work this?" Woody asked, trying to be casual.

Lucas was staring at the wide false front of Barro's mercantile store, which lay on the left side of the street between the hotel and the Straight Shot. "I'm thinkin' about it."

"I could go down to the stables," Woody said, "and pick up that bag of feed, while you're in Barro's."

"Feed's heavy," Lucas said. "We can get that when we're through in the mercantile."

What he was really saying, Ruel knew, was that they'd better stay together. If Woody got the point, he gave no sign of it.

"I can handle a bag of feed," he said, climbing down off the wagon and walking away.

Ruel thought for an instant Lucas would call him back. Woody was visibly nervous as he neared McLouth and his companions. They watched him in beady-eyed silence as he turned in under the stable arch and out of their sight.

Lucas drove on down to the mercantile. Leaving his wagon at the rack, he entered the building, not hurrying and not dawdling.

McLouth and his men posted themselves under the Straight Shot's awning, watching the mercantile and the stable runway by turns.

From somewhere above and behind Ruel came the plantive *croo-ah, croo, croo* of a dove. The song was repeated. A brown dog skulked along the litter-strewn gutter, pausing to sniff at the ground, then turned into an alley.

Two small boys came along the plank walk, cuffing and wrestling each other off balance. A door opened; a woman spoke to them. They turned, wide-eyed, for an ⌐pen-mouthed stare at McLouth. They were still staring as the woman herded them into the building.

There was nobody on the street now, Ruel saw, but himself and the Y Lightning trio.

Lucas came out of the store and deposited a pair of bulging brown-paper bags in the wagon. He made a second trip, with a sales clerk to help him. He climbed up on the wagon's box seat and sat waiting, acting as if he hadn't a care in the world.

Woody stepped out from the stable runway with a sack of feed slung over his shoulder. As he came along the street McLouth said something to him. Woody stiffened. His stride faltered, then he kept going.

McLouth waved his companions down off the plank walk. They stepped around in front of Woody, blocking his way. Woody tried to go around them. One of them tripped him, while another pushed him.

Woody's ankle turned under him as he staggered, handicapped by that bag of feed on his shoulder. He dropped the load and turned on his tormentors, a wild anger in his eyes. McLouth smiled, and said something out of the side of his mouth, inclining his head toward Woody's gun.

Lucas said, "Woody, let that feed go. Come up here."

For a moment Woody stood trembling in indecision. Turning his back on the killer, he plodded up the street to where Lucas waited. McLouth's mouth curled. He followed Woody up toward the wagon and stood watching Lucas, a devil's half smile on his face.

"Where you goin' with that?" he asked, indicating the wagon.

"C Bar?"

"You don't hear so good, Wright," said the gunfighter. "You ain't haulin' no supplies to C Bar."

"I think I am, if I need them, and have the money to buy them."

McLouth's eyes shuttled toward Ruel, then he glanced back over his shoulder to make sure his men were with him. He climbed up into the bed of the wagon and began to shove Lucas's purchases out over the tailgate, which had not been lifted.

A sugar bag split as it landed, and spilled its contents onto the hoof-pocked, manure-littered street. A month's supply of potatoes rolled every which way. A carton of eggs struck the ground with a sickening plop.

Lucas's face was fire-red. He looked as if he were about to explode. That's what McLouth wants, Ruel thought. He's tryin' to make Lucas go for his gun.

Ruel knew he could not sit here on the porch rail, like a bump on a log, and see Jean's father butchered. He walked toward the wagon.

McLouth, as Ruel approached, struck a pose in the wagon bed, spreading his legs, resting freckled hands on his hips. His lips pulled away from tobacco-stained teeth. His eyes never left Ruel's

Ruel didn't stop until he'd come abreast of the wagon, close enough to reach out and touch the black mare standing between the shafts.

"Get down, McLouth," he said.

McLouth fell into a flex-kneed crouch and smiled the way he had smiled at Con Wishard, his eyes saying, "Make me."

Ruel fumbled, with no apparent purpose, at the knotted ends of his bandanna. As the cloth came undone, he flicked it away from his neck, and stung the mare on the hip with it. The animal stepped forward, jerking the wagon out from under McLouth's skidding feet.

The gunman cursed as he was dumped into the street. He was trying, Ruel saw, to get his gun out.

Ruel grabbed his arm and shook it, at the same time slamming him back against the wagon. McLouth's gun dropped to the ground. Ruel's hand was on his own gun as he stepped back now. "Tell your friends to stand hitched, McLouth."

"Why should I?"

Ruel spoke to Lucas. "Keep an eye on them, will you?"

"Sure." Lucas's eyes narrowed on McLouth's companions, as if daring them to try something. They stood there in sullen uncertainty as Ruel, after kicking McLouth's gun aside, drew his own gun and tossed it away.

McLouth stared at him an incredulous instant. He

grinned and came toward Ruel, running in his eagerness for this fight.

Ruel impaled him on a long left. McLouth, accepting the punch as a minor annoyance, came boring in, pummeling Ruel in the body.

It was hard, Ruel found, not to groan at the pain. His broken ribs had not healed completely. And he was not strong. Make this fast, he thought. And to hell with the rules.

McLouth dropped his head and came at him in another bulllike rush. Ruel stepped aside. He put his leg out, tripping the gunman. As McLouth fell, Ruel brought the heel of his hand down on the back of the man's neck. McLouth, stunned by the blow, came surging up sooner than he ought to have. He started to throw punches wildly.

Ruel held him off with the left, awaiting his chance to move in. When it came, he hooked his right hand into the gunman's midsection.

McLouth bent forward, grimacing. Ruel brought his knee up against the man's forehead. McLouth went staggering back against the mercantile's tie-rail, and bounced glancingly off it.

For a moment, the black mare's tie-rope, catching him at the shoulder blades, kept him from falling. The horse reared, whinnying and lifting its forefeet, taking up slack and throwing McLouth off the rope.

Ruel hit him, and he went down. He was not out, Ruel saw, but he seemed to have lost interest in his surroundings.

"I thought he was tough," Ruel said to McLouth's companions.

"He is," one of them said. "You'll find out."

Ruel's eyes crinkled with a brittle amusement as he bent to pick up his gun. He watched McLouth's partners half carry the gunman along the plank walk toward the Straight Shot, then he turned toward Lucas.

"Better get rolling," he murmured. He helped them to reload the wagon.

Lucas, as he gathered the reins, said in a voice thick with emotion, "Son, I don't know what to say."

"Say 'Giddap,'" Ruel grinned. He indicated Lucas's purchases in the wagon. "Sooner you get to C Bar with this stuff, the better."

"You be all right?" Lucas frowned.

"Sure." Ruel watched the rig roll away from him as Lucas slapped the mare with the reins. He could feel people watching him now from behind partly closed doors and half-drawn window blinds. He had never felt more alone.

He put his horse up at the livery stable, breakfasted at Pearl's Cafe, had a bath, a shave, and a haircut, and hired himself a room. He idled the afternoon away out on the hotel porch, staring challengingly at the swing doors of the Straight Shot saloon, which was Y Lightning's headquarters, he had been told, here in Chenango.

He went up to bed after supper. Along toward midnight he was awakened by a crackle of gunfire down in the street. Standing at the window, peering obliquely down, he saw half a dozen men reel drunkenly along the plank walk.

One of them lifted his gun and shot at the moon, while a second man sighted on an easier target, somebody's upstairs' window. All six of them laughed as shards of broken glass cascaded down.

Ruel went back to bed, cursing mildly. Twice more, in as many hours, he was awakened by drunken shouts and intermittent gunfire. In the small hours of the morning, someone knocked at his door.

He struck a match to the oil lamp, pulled his gun out from under his pillow, pancaked himself against the wall, and used his foot to ease the door open. A rumpled little man with tired eyes in a round red face poked his head in, eying Ruel up and down.

"You can put that away," he said. "My name's Anders. I'm a doctor."

Ruel tossed his gun on the bed. "What's on your mind, Doc?"

"May I come in?"

"Come ahead." He waved his guest toward the room's only chair, and waited to hear how he rated a visitor at this hour.

"I'm here on this town's behalf, son. We're in trouble, and I've got a hunch you can help us."

"Oh?" Ruel said. "How?"

"You had any experience rodding the law? Don't smile, man. This is no smiling matter." Doc Anders hesitated. "Haven't you heard about Con Wishard?"

"You mean the marshal? What about him?"

"He's quit."

"Quit?" Ruel found it hard to believe that Wishard had turned in his badge.

"He's left town already," Doc said.

"How?" Ruel frowned. "He'd be in no shape to ride, Doc."

"He left on the train. I can't say I blame him. He'll never regain full use of his arm. And he's a little old to teach himself to shoot with the left hand."

"Speakin' of shootin', who's been makin' all the noise down on the street, Doc?"

"Y Lightning. They're celebrating the fact that Con Wishard's left town. That was quite a job you did on McLouth, son." Doc Anders took a star-shaped badge from his pocket. "Speaking for the responsible citizens of this town, I'd be pleased if you'd pin this on."

"That's not for me," Ruel said.

"Our local businessmen figure they have a stake in this town. They'll ante up to protect it. I can offer you—"

"I'd as soon not know what you can offer," Ruel said.

"There are a lot of decent, law-abiding folks here in Chenango, son. They're in trouble. What's happened tonight is only a sample of what we can expect from Frank Gant's hoodlum crew, with Wishard out of the picture. It wouldn't take many nights like last night to make a ghost town of Chenango."

"Didn't Wishard have a deputy?" Ruel asked.

Doc shook his head morosely. "I won't paint a false picture for you, son. Frank Gant's a born bully. He'd like to be able to crack the whip here in town. Whoever pins this badge on is asking for trouble. You've a right to know what you'd be getting into."

"That's no job for me, Doc."

"Why not?"

Ruel eased down on the bed. "Say for personal reasons."

The little man in the rumpled suit looked at him with a frown. "I'm a doctor, Matheson. I spend half my time hearing confessions, helping people thrash out their problems. If it's something you'd care to talk about—"

"Thanks, Doc. It isn't."

The smaller man sighed. He gave a weary wag of his head. "Well, if you won't wear the badge, maybe there's another way you could help."

"How?"

"Stay on out there at C Bar." He saw Ruel's brow start to furrow, and said, "You wouldn't be helping just Lucas. You'd be helping Yancey Jefford hold his little spread west of town. And—"

"All I know about Yancey Jefford," Ruel said, "is that Lucas can beat him at checkers. What do I owe him?"

"Owe him?"

"That's right. And while we're on the subject, what do I owe Lucas? Seems to me I've paid any debt I ever owed C Bar."

Doc Anders' face stiffened. He rose, walked to the door, and stood with his hand on the knob, regarding Ruel. "I don't suppose you're aware of the fact that Lucas's girl saved your life."

"You mean by her nursin'?" Ruel asked, lifting quizzical eyebrows.

The doctor's mouth twisted. "The night you dragged into C Bar more dead than alive, she climbed in bed with you and thawed you out. She saved your life as surely as if she'd pulled you out of quicksand. If she hadn't had sense enough to flaunt the conventions, you wouldn't be here now."

"I—I didn't know, Doc."

Naturally." The Doc's eyes were scornful. "It's not the kind of thing Jean would mention. I'd think about it, if I were in your place."

"Look, Doc," Ruel stammered, "I—"

"Think about it," Doc said over his shoulder as he walked out. The door clicked shut. Ruel sat there on the hard narrow bed, staring at nothing.

So she crawled in with me. No wonder I made it. He grinned, picturing himself and Jean under the covers. She had saved his life. He wondered what he could do to repay her for that, and his grin faltered.

9

Frank Gant touched the mare's flank with the whip. The buggy moved along the street smartly. Passing Barro's store, where McLouth, earlier this week, had tried and failed to prevent Lucas Wright from leaving town with a load of supplies, Frank felt a deep and bitter frustration.

He used the whip on the mare again. His mother turned on the buggy's seat, glancing up at him.

"What's the hurry, Frank? We're early."

Frank let the mare run.

"For goodness' sake, Frank, slow down. You're taking me to church, not a fire."

Frank paid her no attention. Townspeople moved along the plank walks, the women in their Sunday finery, the men in somber black. None of them seemed to want to meet his eye, Frank noticed. These people had been catching hell, for the past several days, from his crew. Frank felt their animosity toward him.

From up the street came a heavy, insistent clangor of church bells. Frank's lip curled.

His mother said, "What's so amusing?" Frank didn't answer and she fussed at her hair. "Is my hat straight?" she asked.

Frank didn't look at her.

"What are you smiling about?" she asked. "What's so funny?"

"It just come to me what those bells are saying."

"What?"

"Ding dong, ding dong; come on, moron."

His mother's face seemed to freeze. Her small, under-shot jaw closed like a trap. "That isn't amusing. If you must scoff at religion, you might choose a better time for it."

Frank grinned. His mother glanced over her shoulder and said, "We're raising dust, Frank. If you'd think about anyone but yourself, you'd realize it. Slow down, won't you?"

It was true, Frank saw. The street was overlain by a fine dry powder. A slight breeze was carrying dust kicked up by the mare across to the plank walk. Frank saw annoyance in the eyes of some of the better-dressed women. He saw open hostility in the eyes of their male escorts, and the thought, Look out. There's a limit to what this town'll take, even from you.

He fingered the specimen of coal in his pocket. Wait'll I start mining that ridge north of C Bar. I'll be a millionaire in less'n a year. I'll be able to buy this jerk town and everyone in it. Nobody better look cross-eyed at me then.

Grinning inwardly, he reined down to a trot, then to a walk as he turned into the churchyard. Knots of people stood talking idly in the shade of the elms. Some heads turned Frank's way, but nobody gave him a greeting. It came to Frank, with a little shock of surprise and annoyance, that he was being given the silent treatment.

Well, he had never had a thin skin. He could take it. He climbed down, helped his mother out of the buggy, gave her his arm, and escorted her as far as the church door.

"Why do you bother, Frank?" she asked.

"Bother? With what?"

"Putting on such a show."

Her superior manner amused him. Nobody knew better than Frank what she was, a coal miner's widow who'd lived on a son-in-law's charity for years until she'd come to stay with Frank at Y Lightning.

She let go of his arm at the door. "Won't you come in with me this once, Frank? I feel so—so conspicuous sitting in that pew alone."

"I'll see you after the sermon."

"It wouldn't hurt you to hear what the parson has to say."

"After," Frank said. He returned to the buggy and

drove back toward the center of town. He was remembering the day he'd driven his mother out to the ranch from the depot, how her eyes had bugged at sight of Y Lightning's huge masonry house and well-kept outbuildings.

He'd wanted her, and his sister back East, to know he'd come up in the world. His mother had been impressed, until she learned how he'd got where he was—not through hard work, but through marriage.

He had come abreast of the Straight Shot which, for appearances' sake, kept its doors shut Sunday mornings. Frank left his buggy at the rack and picked his way along a debris-littered alley to the rear of the building. He thumped on the door with the heel of his hand and was admitted, finally, by the proprietor, bald Ralph Willis.

"About time," Frank said.

"Sorry, Frank. I was lyin' down." The saloon keeper's voice was aggrieved. "Your bunch was in again last night, shootin' holes in my woodwork, actin' as ornery as they know how. They're gonna ruin this town."

"They're good boys," Frank said. "They're just letting off steam."

"I wish they'd let it off somewhere else. I never got rid of them till four in the mornin'."

Frank looked at the man. "You like the color of their money all right, don't you, Ralph?"

"Well, sure, sure. Don't get me wrong. I ain't sayin' they ain't welcome in my place. It's just—"

Frank, stepping up to the bar, said, "It's a dusty drive in here from Y Lightning. My throat's dry."

"Why, sure, Frank. Sure." The bald man placed a shot glass and a bottle of whiskey on the bar in front of Frank.

Frank poured himself a drink and nodded down at the bottle. "What about you?"

"If you don't mind, Frank, I'd as soon not start the day off with this stuff. I ain't had nothing to eat yet."

"I do mind," Frank said. "Man likes company when he drinks."

The bald man was obviously suffering from lack of sleep and a headache. He said hopefully, "I'll have a beer with you."

"Come on, Ralph, come on," Frank said, indicating the bottle.

Ralph Willis produced a second shot glass from beneath the bar and poured whisky into it from the bottle. "I don't guess a hair of the dog'll kill me."

He downed his drink quickly, grimacing. Frank, watching over the brim of his own lifted glass, smiled.

"Have another."

"No thanks. That's all my stomach'll stand," Ralph said.

Frank shrugged. Ralph, he could tell, was only waiting for him to leave, so he could tumble back into bed. Frank stayed the better part of an hour, helping himself to a drink occasionally from the bottle. He kept urging the saloon keeper to join him, subjecting the man to a kind of civilized torture.

He left when he began to feel the effect of the whisky, and drove back to the church to wait for his mother. He pulled the buggy to a halt in the shade of a willow. Several church windows were open for coolness. He could hear the preacher's voice droning, and he felt a reedy annoyance.

He'd be damned, Frank thought, if he'd ante up when the plate was passed, like those fools inside there, in payment for being harangued by an old windbag.

He could pick out an occasional word, but no more from where he sat. Having nothing better to do, he stepped down and crossed the yard, posting himself beneath an open window.

He heard the preacher refer to "certain disruptive elements in the community, who shall be nameless . . ." He heard him speak of "persons who covet what belongs to their neighbors . . . " and of "our need and desire to live in peace with one another, in accordance with God's will. . . . " He heard: "Let us pray that God, in His wisdom, will favor our parched earth with rain, so that the dumb animals He has placed in our keeping need not suffer for lack of water. Let us pray that any misguided soul who hopes to gather unto himself a disproportionate share of this world's goods, at the expense of his neighbors, will see the error of his ways."

The preacher was winding his sermon up now, Frank

74

sensed. He returned to the buggy. He had bit the end off a cigar, and was sitting there champing angrily on it when the congregation spilled out into the churchyard.

A group of children came first, scrambling in their eagerness; then came the church members, each pausing at the door for a word with the preacher.

Frank's gorge rose at the sight of the skinny old man in his high white collar, and he thought, I ought to break you in half, you old fossil. That whisky he'd taken was making him reckless, he realized. I better get away from here before I do somethin' foolish.

He watched impatiently for his mother. She came out at last practically arm in arm with Jean Wright. The girl's father was one step behind, walking with that big gray wolf, Yancey Jefford, and his tiny woman. Woody Yarmon and Ruel Matheson came out of the church now.

Frank felt something twist and tighten within him at sight of the man who had mopped up the street with Harry McLouth. He went over and spoke to his mother.

"Let's go."

His mother looked at him the way she had looked at him years ago, when he'd done something she disapproved of. "Don't be rude, Frank."

"Come on."

"In a moment." She went on with what she'd been saying to Lucas Wright's girl. She'd never defied him before, Frank thought. It gave him an odd, uncomfortable feeling inside.

"I said come on. I have things to do, if you haven't."

"Sakes alive, Frank, wait in the buggy. A few minutes won't kill you."

He felt like giving her the flat of his hand. He would have, if they'd been alone. He turned toward Lucas.

"This man working for you now, Lucas?" he asked, indicating the drifter.

"Why?"

"Could go hard on you if he is. McLouth's got a score to settle with him."

Yancey Jefford said, "I guess it's for Lucas to say who works for him."

75

Frank scowled at the tall, stoop-shouldered rancher. "When I want your advice, I'll ask for it."

Yancey Jefford straightened to his full six feet, three inches. As he opened his mouth to reply his wife touched his elbow. "Come along, Yancey."

The tall, gray-haired man shook his head. "I got somethin' to say first."

"Come along." The woman stood no taller than her husband's shoulder, but it was clear that her will was the stronger. As Yancey Jefford allowed her to lead him away, Lucas Wright, embarrassed for his friend, glared at Frank.

Ruel Matheson's eyes were focused on Frank's. "I work for C Bar, since you ask. And here's some advice, friend. Stay clear of that outfit."

Frank stared at the man. "You tellin' me what to do?"

"You, and every man workin' for you."

Frank ground his teeth, thinking, Mister, I ought to beat the living hell out of you again. Something in Matheson's eyes damped off his anger. He would not gain title to C Bar, he reminded himself, by engaging in a churchyard brawl with this fellow.

Woody Yarmon was standing with one arm around the girl, as if to shield her from unpleasantness. Frank, whose wife had been dead for a year, felt a stir of interest, a tingle of desire as he eyed the girl. Woody Yarmon wasn't man enough for a girl like her, Frank thought. He almost regretted the dream of empire which had brought on his quarrel with her and her father.

He saw Matheson smile reassuringly at the girl, and thought, Well, he's gone on her too. Why else would he stay on at C Bar? He could feel his antagonism toward the man deepen.

"No damn cowhand can tell me what to do, friend."

"You've been told," Matheson said. "Stay away from C Bar."

Frank could feel his fingers curling into his palms. It went against his grain to let any man tough-talk him in public. But as a man who had earned his living at poker, he knew that it was necessary, at times, to give up a small pot in order to win the last one—the big one.

"You ready?" he said to his mother. He led her across the yard. She had to ask him to hand her up to the buggy seat; he was thinking about that damned drifter.

"Next time I'm ready to leave and you ain't," he said on the way out of town, "I'll leave without you."

"Yes. I believe you'd do that, Frank."

"What was that between you and the girl?"

"Why?"

"Goddamit, I'm askin' you," Frank said.

"Don't blaspheme on the Lord's day, Frank. We were socializing. She's nice. I suppose she sensed that I felt neglected, and decided she'd better speak to me."

"Hell! Ain't you dry back of the ears? She's toadyin' up to you, hopin' you'll get me off her old man's back."

"You're too cynical, Frank, if you think that. Jean isn't that sort."

"She's Lucas's daughter. You keep away from her."

"I won't do that. Not in return for a kindness."

"Keep away from her."

His mother turned on the seat, looking up at Frank. Her small chin was thrust outward. There was a stubborn gleam in her eyes.

Frank said, "I'm askin' you not to hobnob with people I'm fightin'. If that's askin' too much, we'll forget these trips to town, Sunday mornings."

"You mean—stop coming to church, Frank?"

He nodded.

"I can't give up coming to church, Frank. I've attended church all my life. It's my only pleasure."

"Then if I was you I'd mend my ways."

His mother looked searchingly at him. "What ails you, Frank? Why can't you let people live their own lives?"

"I don't know what you're talkin' about."

"I think you do. You were the same way as a boy. Always bullying the other children, taking their things. And now it's the Wrights. You haven't changed, have you?"

"Do you ever quit gabbin'?" Frank asked. She had reminded him how things had been for him years ago, back in Shamokin. He could remember the rude, unpainted shanty he had grown up in; he could smell the coal dust in the air, and feel the grit coal left on the hands.

When his father, who'd never been anything but a coal cracker, had contracted consumption and started coughing up blood, Frank had taken his place in the mine. He'd soon had a bellyful of that. One dark night he'd slipped out of the house, after helping himself to what rainy-day money his mother'd been able to lay aside; and, following Horace Greeley's advice, he had come West.

Years later, after a particularly good run of luck at the card tables, he had sent that money back to his mother. She'd written him by the next mail, to thank him, but Frank could never convince himself that his belated gesture had bought her forgiveness.

He felt a moment's regret for his decision to let her come to live with him at Y Lightning. The prospect of having her underfoot indefinitely filled him with resentment.

"Anytime you're not happy here," he said, "you can go back where you come from."

"I won't sponge on your sister and her husband again, Frank. I lived with them fourteen years. You know how little he earns in the mine."

"You sayin' you want to stay here?"

"I have no choice." His mother spoke in a small, half-ashamed voice, as though she hated to make the admission.

"You better learn what side your bread's buttered on," Frank said. "Keep your nose out of what don't concern you."

He cracked his whip over the mare's swinging flanks, lifting her to a run. His mother grasped the arm rest, steadying herself in the narrow seat. She looked smaller and skinnier, more like a cadaver, Frank thought, than ever.

10

On the way out to C Bar after church service, Woody Yarmon kept glancing at Ruel Matheson, who was keeping pace with the carriage on horseback. He's got guts. He sure told Frank off, Woody thought. But he had seen the wicked highlights in Frank Gant's eyes, back there in the churchyard. He wasn't about to thank Ruel for rousing Frank's anger.

I ought to ask for my time, Woody thought, and shake dust on this country. What's to keep me at C Bar?

Jean, he thought, and he turned for an appraising glance at her. She was staring straight ahead, preoccupied with her own troubled thoughts, he guessed. He caught his breath at her beauty.

That was the way she'd affected him the first time he saw her, his first day at C Bar. One look, and it had been all over for him. He hadn't let on how he felt. He'd mooned over the girl for months without tipping his hand, until Frank Gant started to get tough with Lucas, and Lucas's crew decided to quit him.

Frank had told them they'd be "better off somewhere else," whatever that meant. Woody, after a long debate with himself, decided to stay on.

"You needn't, you know," Jean told him. "You don't owe us that, Woody."

"I'm not quitting," he said. This was in the privacy of C Bar's kitchen, and she stood on tiptoes and kissed him.

"What's that for?" he asked, his heart thumping so loudly he was sure she must hear it.

"Thanks," Jean said.

Woody wanted to put his arms around her, but was afraid if he did she would push him away. She came into

79

his arms without any urging, and stood with her head pressed against his shoulder.

"Woody, I'm scared. Not for myself. For Dad. Frank Gant's such a—a scorpion. And that crew of his. Ugh!"

She was crying. Woody could feel the sobs wrench at her as she stood against him. He curled a finger under her chin, kissing the tears from her eyes, and then he kissed her on the mouth, gently.

She didn't respond, nor did she pull away. He had achieved an intimacy he hadn't hoped for. He knew that Jean was distraught, that he'd caught her at an unguarded moment. But he had kissed her. And maybe next time she would kiss back.

There had been no next time. The worsening situation between Frank Gant and her father was no backdrop for romance. Memory of her kiss—of the way she'd felt in his arms—made it hard to be patient.

He glanced at her covertly now. She likes me, he thought. She'd never've let me kiss her if she didn't. Unless she was just feelin' grateful. I don't want her if that's all she feels toward me. Hell I don't, who'm I kiddin'? I want her so bad I choke up every time I look at her.

But damn it, what about Frank? He's gonna start bashin' heads in now.

For ten minutes, as the carriage carried him and Jean and her father along the gravel road, Woody sat silent, thinking. The product of his thinking was not apparent until that afternoon when he and Jean took a walk out C Bar's lane.

"You ask me," he said, "Frank Gant's made his position plenty clear. He wants our grass. One way or another, he'll have it."

"One way or another?"

Woody picked up a handful of pebbles and flipped them, one by one, off his thumbnail. "It's like you said. Frank ain't hardly human. He's more like some kind of wild animal. The way things are around here now, with a do-nothin' sheriff at the other end of the county, and no marshal in Chenango—all I'm sayin' is I don't like the picture. Frank's a bully, and—"

"I know," Jean said. "Ruel could tell us about that."

Her expression softened as she mentioned Ruel's name. "What are you getting at, Woody?" she asked.

"I'm wonderin' if the game's worth the candle. You got to be practical in a situation like this."

"Practical?"

"Your father's riskin' his life tryin' to hang onto range that's too dry for cattle."

He saw the puzzlement in Jean's eyes. "Our range wasn't always dry. We'll have creek water again, if the court rules in Dad's favor."

"Could be next year before you get a decision. Meanwhile—" Woody shrugged. "Are you sure you're doin' what's right, hangin' on here?"

"Dad's sure." Jean looked both proud and concerned as she added, "Dad says when you fight for your rights you're fighting for everybody's rights. And it's true. Someone has to stop Frank Gant before he's too big to stop, Woody."

"Maybe he's too big already."

"Maybe. But we have Ruel on our side now."

Her voice softened, it seemed to Woody, as she spoke Matheson's name.

"I'm not sure Dad *could* quit," Jean said. "I have a feeling there wouldn't be enough money left for another start, if C Bar gets away from us."

Woody thought about that. Pulse pounding at the thought of what he was about to suggest, he said, "I got some money saved. I inherited a little something when my mother died. I been layin' aside as much as I've spent for the better part of twelve years."

"I—I'm afraid I don't see what—"

"Look—" Woody spoke in a rush, knowing no other way to get the words out "—say your dad was to sell C Bar for what's offered, and throw in with me. Between us, we'd have enough to buy another outfit."

Jean's eyes widened at him. "You'd go partners with Dad? But if you've been saving half what you've earned for twelve years, you'd have more to offer than he'd have."

"That don't matter. What matters is we'd still all be together." He felt the blood rush into his cheeks. He stood there, feeling huge and somehow exposed, as though he'd been shoved out onto a stage to be stared at by hundreds of people. He had just proposed to this girl, and he guessed she realized it.

"Look," he said, "you don't have to decide right away. You could think about it, and kind of feel your father out. If he seems agreeable, I'll mention it to him."

"You're sweet." She put her hand on his arm, smiling into his eyes. It was hard, Woody found, to keep his voice level.

"Then you'll speak to your dad?"

"I—I'm not sure. I'll have to think about this first. I'll let you know when I've decided."

"Take your time," he said, swallowing his disappointment.

He didn't sleep much that night. In the morning, he managed a moment alone with Jean as she was preparing breakfast. "You been thinkin' about what I—"

"It's all I've thought about, Woody, since we had our talk."

"What's the verdict?"

"I don't know," she sighed, shaking her head.

She knows what I want, Woody thought. She'd be part of the bargain. She'll go for it, when she's had time to think it over. What she needs is a nudge. One good nudge, and she'll come into my arms.

He hung around the ranch buildings as long as he could after breakfast, but Jean made no overtures toward him. He rode out, finally, for an inspection tour of Lucas Wright's C Bar range. Toward mid-afternoon he reined in alongside a rickety windmill which Ruel Matheson was lashing together, at strategic places, with strips of green cowhide.

Woody hooked a knee over the horn, noting that in this task, as in every task he undertook, Matheson worked with speed and precision. This big, quiet-spoken man seemed to have been born with skills and abilities that other, lesser men acquired only after hours of study and practice.

"Good job you're doin'," Woody murmured. "But ain't you wastin' your effort?"

"I wouldn't have taken this on if I thought so."

"There's no water down that well."

"There will be, once we've had a real rain."

"We won't be here that long."

Ruel looked up. "There's a dim view. What's behind it?"

"You know what shape our critters are in. We got enough water to last them another three or four days. Then what?"

Matheson stared off northward, toward the mountain range that formed the upper boundary of Lucas Wright's range. He said in an apparent change of subject, "What's up there, Woody?"

"Rocks and brush, mostly. Why?"

"Doesn't Lucas make any use of it?"

"Hell, no. It's nothin' but a damn jungle."

"Seems to me there'd have to be *some* moisture up there, to support all that vegetation. How's about riding up there with me, for a look-see?"

"Be a waste of time."

"Maybe," said Ruel. "Let's have a look anyway."

Woody knew his arm was being twisted. Strangely, he didn't resent it. There was something about Ruel he couldn't help warming up to. "Let's go," he said.

They picked their way up into the foothills. A pair of grouse flew up, with an explosive beating of wings, from under Woody's horse's front feet. The animal reared whinnying. Woody had to grab the horn to stay in the saddle.

Overhead, silhouetted against the blue sky, a hawk coasted on spread wings, cutting lazy half circles, then dropped like a stone. Like Frank, Woody thought. That's how he pounces on people.

Halfway up the mountainside they emerged from deep brush into a boulder field. Matheson pulled in, and let his eye swing along the slope, eastward and westward. He pointed toward a cavelike opening under a rock ledge. "What's that?"

Woody lifted his shoulders. "I understand there's some bears up in here."

Ruel climbed down. "No bear dug this cave, Woody."

"Maybe a bobcat," Woody suggested. "Or—"

"A man dug this hole, if you ask me. See those scratch marks on the stone? No claw could have made them. That took metal."

"Who'd be bothered to hack a hole in the mountainside, way to hell-and-gone up here?"

"This was Mex country once," murmured Ruel. "What d' you suppose they used it for mostly? Grazing sheep, maybe?"

"Sheep?" Woody's mouth turned down at the corners.

"I'd give odds a Mex shepherd ran sheep up here years ago."

"Sheep." Woody said, as though the word tasted bad in his mouth.

"Our friend probably got caught in a few rain squalls. He gouged this hole out under the rock for shelter. He was lazy, you'll notice. He didn't dig any more hole than he had to. Now why do you suppose he dug it here rather than somewhere else? Why this location?"

"You tell me," Woody said.

"What's a man on the lookout for when he's got animals to tend, Woody?"

"Grass and water," Woody said without thinking. He stared at Ruel. "You think there's water around here?"

"I'd bet on our long dead friend's laziness." Ruel pivoted slowly, studying the surrounding terrain as though it were a page in a book. After some minutes a cliff swallow swooped downward in flight and disappeared in a tangle of brush.

Ruel broke a limb off a deadfall tree, and used it to beat a crude path through the thicket. Woody tagged along behind, grinning a skeptic's grin.

Then he saw the swallow fly up from beneath a ledge of granite whose bottom surface was dimpled and stained by beads of moisture. Ruel took a jackknife out of his pocket and dug a hole in the soft earth below the ledge.

The blade of the knife was soon stained with mud. In five minutes of digging he had unearthed enough water to slake his thirst on.

"I'm damned," Woody said. "Is there anything you can't figure out, mister?"

"I used to smell out water for a trail herd," Matheson

said. "What's needed here is a V-shaped collecting wall, and some pipe, and a trough."

"You mean there'd be enough water here to help Lucas?"

"More than enough, if it's developed. What's the matter? You look as if you just ate a worm."

"I'm just thinking," Woody said. "Maybe Lucas'd be better off if we didn't tell him."

"Not tell him we found water?"

"That's right." Woody couldn't look Ruel in the eye.

"Why shouldn't we tell him?"

Woody pointed down at the hole Ruel had dug with his knife blade. "I suppose this'd tide us over for a while, but damnit, we're sittin' in a high-stake game with the cards stacked against us. Somebody's goin' to get hurt. It could be you, Ruel. McLouth won't forget that beating you gave him. Frank looked mad enough to kill you, Sunday, up there in the churchyard."

"You tryin' to scare me?" asked Ruel.

"All I'm sayin' is maybe we ought to quit. I'll take my chances when I got no choice. But why risk gettin' killed over an outfit like C Bar?"

"What's really bothering you, Woody?"

"I don't want to commit suicide."

"More to it than that," murmured Ruel.

Woody opened his mouth, intending to blurt out the truth. His pride would not let him mention the suggestion he'd made to Jean. He inclined his head toward the water Ruel had uncovered.

"What do you say, Ruel? Shall we keep quiet about this?"

Ruel shook his head. "When you work for a man like Lucas Wright, you play straight with him," he said.

"You know how Lucas is," Woody said. "He'll never quit, if he figures there's any chance for him against Frank."

"His decision," Ruel said. "Not ours."

Woody swore. His talk with the girl, his offer to throw in with her father, were wasted effort now, thanks to Ruel. On the way down the mountain he kept glancing at Ruel, a cold frustration building inside him.

At one point the game trail they followed crossed a narrow ledge with a sheer granite wall on one side, a hundred-foot drop on the other. Ruel's horse reared suddenly, with no warning whatever, and Ruel had all he could do to keep his place in the saddle.

Woody could see what had frightened the dun. A rattlesnake, aroused and angered by the clatter of hooves on this flinty underfooting, had slithered out from beneath a rock.

At sight of the coiled, tubular body, the beadlike eyes, the tongue flicking in and out of the fanged mouth, Woody reined his own horse in, swallowing.

The snake's tail quivered, making the sound it was named for. The head rose and drew back, ready to strike at the dun's forefeet when they lowered.

Ruel shortened rein, keeping the dun up on his haunches, trying, at the same time, to pull the horse back, away from the rattler.

He fought a losing battle, Woody saw, against the pitch of the ledge and the slick underfooting. The dun, as Woody watched, came close to falling backward over the lip of the ledge.

The thought flicked through Woody's mind that with Ruel out of the way Lucas would not have to know about that water Ruel had discovered. There's no law that says I'd have to tell him.

Ruel was still trying to get his horse under control. He had refused the easy out, which was to slide down from the saddle and let the animal fend for himself.

Woody was suddenly ashamed of the things he had been thinking, of the spectator's role he was playing. He drew his gun, aimed carefully at the snake's head, and squeezed the trigger. He missed, and was lining up on the elusive small target again when Ruel, having brought his horse temporarily under control, whipped his gun from the holster.

No man ever drew and shot a gun under a greater handicap. It occurred to Woody that Ruel shot too quickly, taking no time to aim, and so must waste his bullet.

He saw he was wrong. What had been a rattlesnake, coiled to strike, was something headless—twisting, reflexively writhing. The dread rattling sound, with no intelligence to direct it, ceased abruptly.

Matheson spoke in a quiet voice to the dun. The horse demonstrated confidence in him by easing its feet down.

Woody drew breath past his teeth, whistling, as Matheson reholstered his gun.

"For Christ's sake. Can you do that every time?"

Ruel leaned forward, stroking the dun on the neck. His shoulders rose in a careless gesture. "I luck one off now and then."

"That wasn't luck, Ruel."

Ruel sat there idly, unselfconsciously, his face devoid of expression.

"Where'd you learn to shoot like that?" Woody blurted out at him.

Ruel looked up, a faint annoyance clouding his eyes.

"Let's ride," he said, urging his horse down the trail.

11

Frank Gant, from where he stood on Y Lightning's patio, could see a pall of dust overhanging the basin floor at the foot of C Bar's mountain. He stared at it for some minutes, asking himself what had put that dust there.

He had gone inside for his binoculars, and was peering intently through them when Harry McLouth's voice said, almost at his elbow, "What's up, Frank?"

Frank had no idea where the pock-faced gunman had come from.

"Damn it," he said, "don't Injun up on me that way."

McLouth let out a high-pitched snicker. "Ain't you jumpy this mornin'?" He dipped his head in the direction of Lucas Wright's C Bar holding. "What's so interestin' over there?"

Frank handed the binoculars to him.

"What d' you make of it?" he asked, when McLouth had taken a look.

"That's C Bar's herd makin' that dust, Frank. I'd say they're bein' choused up the side of the mountain. But what in hell for? Where's the point in it?"

Frank debated a moment, then he said, "Suppose you take a *pasear* over there and find out. But don't show yourself to them."

"Why not?"

"Just keep out of sight," Frank said.

"How?"

"Ride a circle and come in from the other side of the ridge. That'll put you above them. You'll see what they're up to. Get going."

McLouth was gone the better part of the morning.

"They found water up on that mountain," he reported on his return. "They've put in a collectin' wall, and a trough. They've drove their whole herd up in there. They can keep their critters alive for weeks on the strength of that water. What's the matter?"

"Nothing." Frank spoke matter-of-factly, as though McLouth's news was of no concern to him, but he was thinking of the coal deposit he had located on C Bar's mountain, and his mood was bitter.

With Lucas Wright's cattle grazing the mountainside, it was only a question of time before Lucas, or one of the men working for him, made the same discovery Frank had made up there.

Frank's fingers closed around the lump of coal in his pocket.

McLouth said, "They'll guard that water like gold, Frank. What's our next move?"

"How in hell should I know?" Frank asked.

"Take it easy," McLouth said.

"What's the matter?"

"Take it easy," the gunman said, looking at him.

Frank grinned. "Don't get tough with me, Harry."

"I don't like nobody takin' that tone with me," said the gunman.

Frank's shrug was an insult. "I'll let you know when I've come up with something," he said.

He waved the man away brusquely.

He was on the patio again an hour later, sitting in deep thought, his chin cupped in his hand, when Jean Wright rode in. She was wearing halfboots, and one of those short-skirted riding habits that had come in style this year. She made a picture pretty enough to frame, Frank thought, noting the rise and fall of her breasts beneath the tailored coat as her horse carried her into the yard. What's she want? What's she doin' here? he thought.

"Howdy?"

"Is Mrs. Gant in?" Jean asked.

Frank's men had come out of the bunkhouse. They stared at Jean Wright now as if they'd never seen a bit of fluff before. Frank glanced at them in annoyance.

"My mother's inside. Climb down," he said, offering the girl a hand.

"I can manage." The hem of her skirt, as she slid down, caught on a stirrup. From across the yard came a catcall, followed by throaty masculine laughter.

Frank saw the color rush to Jean's cheeks. He glared at his men.

"Who's the comedian?" he asked.

They stared innocently into space, grinning like hoodlums.

"All right," Frank said, "you can all get inside."

None of them moved, not even Lute Springer. Frank unleashed his temper at them.

"Move," he said.

They filed sullenly into the bunkhouse. A few brave souls, McLouth among them, posted themselves in the doorway, watching Frank and the girl.

"You'll be more comfortable inside, Miss Wright," Frank said.

The girl walked in ahead of him. Frank's glance, as he followed her, dropped to her well-rounded legs. In the living room, he held a chair for her.

"I'll get my mother," he said, and he left her sitting there with her hands in her lap.

He kept seeing her in his mind's eye as he moved along the hall toward his mother's room. Just thinking about the girl filled him with a tingling excitement. As he neared the old woman's door, he heard her snoring, and gave an intolerant shake of his head, asking himself how so small a woman could make such a racket.

He stood for a moment with his hand on the knob, then returned to the girl without disturbing his mother.

"She was asleep. She'll be along," he said.

The girl looked at him, puzzled, apparently, by the friendliness of his manner.

Frank smiled at her. "Relax," he said. "How would a glass of lemonade strike you, Miss Wright, while you're waiting?"

She regarded him in a reserved, neutral way, and gave a small shake of her head.

90

"It's already made," Frank said. "It's no trouble."

"One glass *would* be refreshing," the girl said.

Frank remembered to excuse himself as he went out. In the kitchen, he poured two lemonades from the pewter pitcher, spiking his glass with a generous portion of hundred-proof whisky.

Returning to the girl, he offered a toast. "To your next visit, Miss Wright."

Her eyes flicked up, then dropped toward her glass. As she drank daintily from it, she glanced at the hallway— Looking for my mother, Frank thought.

"Look," he said, "I don't know why you're here, but—"

"As a matter of fact," the girl said, "I wanted to talk to *you*."

Frank raised a quizzical eyebrow. "If that's the case, why'd you ask for my mother?"

"I thought she might help me persuade you that you don't need my dad's land."

Frank grinned, remembering how sure his mother had been that the girl was too proud to play this role.

"Does Lucas know you're here?" he asked.

Jean shook her head. "If he did he'd never forgive me."

"Then why—"

"Dad's all I have, Mr. Gant. I don't want him killed." Jean's voice broke, and Frank, for one of the few times in his life, felt sympathy for a human being.

"I guess you think I'm an ogre," he said. "People never see but one side of a situation like this. You think I'm playin' you and your father mean, tryin' to ease you off C Bar. Truth is, I'm doin' you a favor."

"A favor?" The girl's mouth sagged.

Frank inclined his head. "There's no chance for Lucas or Yancey Jefford, or any other small operator to make a go of it here in the basin. They've got the deck stacked against them. I don't say that's fair, but that's the way the world is."

"Is that any justification for what you're doing to Dad?"

Frank's mouth tightened. "He has a way out."

"Has he?"

"I made him an offer for C Bar."

"That's right. You offered him less than half what he paid," the girl said.

Frank pretended to be surprised. "He paid too much then. I made him a fair price."

"A *fair* price?" Her voice was bitter.

Frank regarded her thoughtfully. "Suppose I up the ante a thousand."

The girl's eyes widened at him. "Why should you?"

"Why shouldn't I?" Frank lifted his glass to her and drank from it. Oddly, the knowledge that this girl didn't like him made her that much more attractive to him.

She rose uncertainly, and said, "I wonder what's keeping your mother."

"She'll be along," Frank said, rising too now. The whisky made a warm place inside him. Impulsively he walked across the room to the girl and took hold of her arm. She stepped back, frightened by the look in Frank's eyes.

"You don't have to be afraid of me, girlie," Frank said, placing himself between her and the door.

"I'd better be going."

"What's your hurry? I thought you wanted to see the old woman."

"If you don't mind, I'd like to leave."

Frank grasped her shoulders and pulled her off balance toward him. He was surprised at the readiness with which she came into his arms. He was thinking that women were all alike—all basically whores—when the girl twisted violently within his encircling arms and jabbed him in the ribs with her elbow.

He let go of her and stepped back, grunting. He was about to grab her again when she brought her fingernails raking down the side of his face. The pain roused him to a blind fury. He brought his hand up, intending to hit her, and saw an icy contempt in her eyes.

"Go on. I'd expect that of you, Mr. Gant." She made an insult of the "Mister."

Frank moved aside, touching his fingertips to his stinging face. He let her find her own way out to her horse. He stood at the window, watching her leave, and thought, By God, you'll pay. You'll pay for this, girlie.

He was inspecting himself in the mirror over the fireplace when his mother came into the room.

"Merciful heavens, what happened to you, Frank?"

"Nothing."

"Nothing? Why, you look as if a cat had been at your face. Who were you talking to out here?" Frank looked at her, and she said, "I'd swear I heard a woman's voice out here."

"Would you?"

"Was a woman here, Frank?"

"Goddamnit," Frank said. "Get off my back."

His mother's mouth twitched. "If you must use such language, Frank, save it for that riffraff in the bunkhouse. I'm not used to it."

Frank said, "I guess you've heard your share of it."

"Are you calling me a liar?" his mother asked.

"You tryin' to tell me my old man didn't cuss?" Frank asked. "Bullshit."

His mother drew herself up. "I won't listen to such talk."

"You find my talk unpleasant, you can always get away from it."

"How?"

"Go back to Shamokin."

"You mean—live with your sister again?"

"I'll pay your train fare," said Frank, nodding. "If you're worried about bein' a drag on them, I'll send you an allowance—say five dollars a week—after you get there."

He could promise this, Frank thought; he might even send her the money for a while. Anything to get her out of his sight, out of his hair now.

"Well?" he said, too eagerly, and he saw a sharpness come to her eyes.

"I'm not leaving, Frank. It's not that easy. I won't sponge on your sister again. Not when you're so much better able to provide for me here."

"You're forgetting something," Frank said. "You got no say in the matter."

"Are you ordering me out of your house?" asked his mother, staring at him.

A grim humor twisted Frank's mouth.

"What if I say I won't leave, Frank?"

"You can blat about it all you want. You'll leave," said Frank grimly.

"No, Frank. I won't."

"You tellin' me I can't make you?"

His mother looked at him, and Frank saw the willfulness in her eyes. There'd always been a point beyond which you couldn't push her.

"How can you make me, Frank?"

"There's ways."

"How? Are you thinking of tying me hand and foot, and carrying me to the depot in Chenango, with half the town watching?"

"I'll get you there."

"I'm asking you how, Frank."

He didn't dare use force on her. This part of the country didn't go for that sort of thing. If he used his hands on his mother, he wouldn't be safe from his own hard-bitten crew. He stared at her in impotent anger, then he turned and stalked from the room.

Out in the yard he kicked at a tumbleweed, but found no release in the gesture. He saw his men watching him, and turned his head, not letting them see the side of his face that had been scratched.

He walked around behind the house and sat on an old oak stump, his thoughts focusing on Ruel Matheson, a convenient target for his anger. When later he returned to the front of the house, he found Harry McLouth waiting for him.

The gunman pointedly averted his eyes from Frank's face. His head inclined toward C Bar's mountain. "What do you figure we ought to do about that, Frank? You thought about it?"

"There's a couple sticks of dynamite stored in the tool-shed," Frank said musingly, after thinking about it. "Suppose you dig 'em out, Harry."

"Dynamite?" McLouth said.

"Tell the boys to saddle their horses while you're at it. Have Lute catch up that blue roan for me."

McLouth regarded him, pretending not to see the scratch marks on his face. "What're we goin' to do, Frank?"

"We're goin' to blow up a water hole," Frank said. "And you're goin' to kill a man. Now get going."

12

Ruel came awake with all his senses alerted. He could see Lucas Wright curled up in his blankets on the other side of the fire. Above the whisper and crackle of the flames an owl hooted mournfully. Ruel heard his picketed horse stamp the ground.

The night had grown cold as he slept. Only a feeling that something was wrong, that this camp was in danger, could have tempted him to leave his blankets and the warmth of the fire.

He sat up, yawning prodigiously, as he pulled into his boots and strapped his gun on.

Moving in the dark as sure-footedly as a cat, he picked his way downslope toward where Woody Yarmon was standing guard. He had come within fifteen feet of Woody before he was challenged.

"Who is it?" Woody said. "Answer, or—"

"Put that gun away, Woody. It's me, Ruel."

"It ain't right to sneak up on a man that way," complained Woody.

"Maybe it is." One way or another, Frank Gant would try to deprive Lucas's herd of the water in that trough up the slope there. This was war and Woody had better realize it. "Maybe now you'll keep a sharper lookout."

"How was I to know you were there?" Woody grumbled. "You came up on me like a spook."

"All right." Ruel went on down the mountain.

"Anything wrong?" Woody called anxiously. "Where you goin'?"

"Relax," Ruel said. "I'm goin' to look at the moon."

He halted, some hundreds of yards down the slope, and stood for a long time not moving. He knelt presently, and placed his ear against an imbedded rock. He rose, loosened his gun in the holster, and moved on downgrade, choosing his footing with extreme care now.

He could hear horsemen coming toward him, their footfalls cushioned by the needle carpet under the trees. As they came on up the slope, Ruel crouched behind a rock upthrust, holding his breath.

He heard Frank Gant say, "What's that glow up there?"

Harry McLouth's raspy voice said, "That'll be their campfire. What're you aimin' to do, Frank?"

Frank Gant broke a long silence, saying, "I want that camp destroyed."

McLouth said, "They must've posted a guard. How we goin' to get close enough to—"

"Your problem," Frank said. "You can take six men with you, Harry. Make sure you get Matheson. Don't come back down here until Matheson's dead."

Ruel caught his breath. There was a humor, of a sort, in this situation, but who smiles at his own death warrant? He heard McLouth name six men and lead them cautiously up the slope. Frank, and the two men who'd stayed with him, climbed off their horses. Frank sat on the half-rotted trunk of a deadfall tree; his men perched on a tilted rock. All three were silent—sobered, apparently, by the thought of McLouth and his grisly errand.

Ruel didn't move. He was thinking of Lucas and Woody up the slope there, thinking that he ought to be doing something for them. Frank and his men stared up the slope, more interested in McLouth's whereabouts now than in their own whispered comments.

Ruel eased himself prone to the ground and slithered toward them. If I could work in close enough to get the drop on them. This better come off though—God help me if I don't bring this thing off.

Dragging himself along the ground, he came up on Frank from behind, and rammed his gun against Frank's back.

"Don't move," he said.

He heard the big man catch his breath. "Who is it?"

Ruel curled an arm around Frank's muscular neck,

rammed the gun harder against him. "You want to live, Gant?"

"Sure. Who doesn't?"

"Tell your men to keep their hands off their guns."

Frank Gant said, "Better play along with him, boys."

"Tell them to drop their gunbelts and back away from them," Ruel said.

"You heard the man, boys."

Ruel heard a whisper of friction, a heavy thud as one belt dropped. The second belt, when it hit the ground, made less noise. Peering through the darkness toward its owner, Ruel caught the glint of gun metal.

"Drop it," he said. The man let go of the gun as though it were burning his fingers.

"What kind of eyes you got?" he grumbled.

Ruel eased Frank's gun from the holster.

"Cup your hands to your mouth, Gant," he said. "Start yelling."

"What's the idea?"

"Tell your men up the slope that if anything happens to Lucas or Woody—"

An explosion up the mountainside drowned out Ruel's words. There was a flashing white light, a crash as of thunder. Somebody yelled, "Watch out!" and presently Ruel, through the ringing in his ears, made out the sound of a boulder hurtling downgrade. Judging from the racket it made, it was big and heavy enough to flatten anything in its path.

Frank Gant said, "Let's get out of here." The big man was about to make a break for his freedom.

"That'll pass left of us," Ruel said. "I'll shoot the first thing that moves. That means you, Gant."

The boulder came down the slope, crashing through brush and small trees. It passed them on the left, and now Ruel pointed Frank Gant's gun at the sky and pulled trigger three times. He heard McLouth and his gang coming at a run in response to that summons.

He waited until they'd come within hailing distance.

"Hold it, McLouth."

McLouth's party reined in. McLouth's voice, edged with caution, said, "Who is it?"

"I've got a gun rammed against your boss's back. Tell the man how things are for you, Gant."

"How are they?"

"Guess," Ruel said. He put more pressure behind the gun. He could feel the big man arch his back away from the weapon.

"Don't do anything rash, boys," Frank Gant said.

"That's better," Ruel said. "Tell them to make themselves scarce. Tell them to ride back where they came from."

"What about me?"

"You'll stay."

"The hell I will."

Ruel jabbed the man with his gun. "You any idea how big a hole a forty-five slug would rip in you, Gant?"

"You're not goin' to shoot."

"No?" Ruel said.

"You're not that hard," the big man said.

"I heard the orders you gave McLouth a few minutes ago," Ruel said.

The big man took a moment to think about that.

"Ride back to the ranch, boys."

"Huh?" McLouth said.

"You heard me," Frank growled. "Ride back." McLouth still protested, but Frank Gant silenced him with a curse. "Move," he said, "when I tell you something."

They moved. Ruel waited until he could no longer hear them picking their way down the grade; then, still poking Frank with the gun, he walked the big man up the mountain.

Lucas Wright's voice, tinged with hysteria, challenged them before they reached the campfire. "Don't move, or by God I'll gut-shoot the pair of you."

"Simmer down, Lucas. Doesn't sound like you're hurt," Ruel said drily.

"What hurts me is I didn't plug one of those bastards. Who's with you?"

"Neighbor of yours."

"A neighbor?"

"Evenin', Lucas," Frank Gant said.

Woody Yarmon spoke from the darkness somewhere behind Lucas. "Who is it, Ruel?"

"Fetch me a rope," Ruel said. He tied Frank Gant's hands behind him when a rope had been brought, explaining, as he worked at the knot, how he happened to have the big man in tow.

Lucas said in a high, throaty voice, "Bring him over alongside the fire."

"What for?"

"I'm goin' to shoot the son of a bitch. I want to see the look in his eyes when I pull the trigger."

"Take it easy," Ruel said.

"Easy my eye. I'm goin' to shoot him."

"An unarmed man? Cut it out, Lucas. Keep away from that fire."

"What for?"

"One of his men could be skulking around. There's a hero in every outfit."

"All right," Lucas said. "I'll shoot him right here."

Ruel said, "Come off it."

"You think I won't shoot him? After what's happened tonight I'd as soon shoot him as step on an ant."

"That's temper talking."

Lucas turned and flung an order into the shadows behind him. "Fetch another rope down here, Woody."

"Wh—what for?" Woody asked.

"More'n one way to stomp a snake."

Woody moved away, somewhat reluctantly, as though he didn't care for his errand. Frank Gant said, in the cool, even voice of a man who has learned self-discipline at the card tables, "Any idea how much hell my crew'll raise, Lucas, if I'm not back at Y Lightning inside of two hours?"

"How much hell is that?" Lucas asked, with sarcasm.

"I got a hard bunch ridin' for me."

Lucas snorted. "You suggestin' they'd be loyal to you after you're dead?"

Frank's sullen pride held him silent. He was not going to beg. Ruel felt a grudging admiration for the man's courage. He wished suddenly he had not brought Frank here.

Woody returned with the rope Lucas had asked for. Lucas offered it to Ruel, murmuring, "Can you make a hang noose?"

Ruel backed away, avoiding contact with the rope.

"Word with you, Lucas." Drawing the old man aside, he said in a voice that discouraged eavesdropping, "Deal me out. I don't want any part of a hanging."

"Could a man ask why?" the old man murmured after a moment.

Ruel hesitated. "It's—kind of personal. Oh, all right, you're entitled to know. My—my father died that way."

"On a hang rope?" Lucas's voice was shocked, and sympathetic. "I didn't mean to pry, son. I'm just so damned mad I don't hardly know what I'm doing. Why don't you hightail it back to the ranch?"

"What about you and Woody?"

"We'll be along, when we've done what needs doing."

Ruel shuddered, and a voice inside him said, Don't let him do it. Talk him out of it. But another voice took exception. It's for him to decide. In a way you can't blame him, after what Frank's done to him.

Ruel picked his way through the dark to his tethered horse. He had let Lucas down, he supposed as he rode out. When he raised C Bar's buildings, he was thinking steadily of Frank Gant, of the fate that had overtaken the big man. He thought, If I wake Jean up riding in, she'll want to know what's goin' on.

He climbed down a quarter mile out, and walked the dun in, off-saddling in the pasture. He stowed his gear in the shed and crept into the bunkhouse, feeling like a sneak and a coward.

He was lying in his bunk wide awake, an hour later, when Lucas and Woody rode in. Lucas went into the house. Woody, after off-saddling both horses, came tramping into the bunkhouse. He struck a match to the candle in the sardine can, saw the question in Ruel's eyes, and said, "We didn't hang him. When it came to the pinch we couldn't go through with it."

"Oh?" Ruel was both relieved and disturbed by this information. "I thought sure Lucas would—"

"You know how he is. He blows hot, he blows cold.

Time he'd got a noose made to suit him, and put it round Frank's neck, he'd begun to cool off. So when Frank offered to bury the hatchet and undam the White-woman—"

"Frank said he'd do that?"

"He swore up and down there'd be water in our end of the crick before noon tomorrow."

Ruel's lips pursed. His brow furrowed. "Where is he?"

"Who?"

"Frank. Where's Frank now?"

Woody's eyes dropped toward the bunkhouse floor. "At Y Lightning. We—let him go."

"Let him go?" Ruel said. "Then what makes you think he'll make good—"

"We took a chance." Woody saw Ruel's pained expression. "Look, if we'd held him till the dam was down, he could build another as soon as we let him loose, couldn't he? We figured we might as well trust him."

"Trust him? Trust Frank Gant?"

"Why not? What did we have to lose?" For an instant Woody's eyes met Ruel's, then they fell away.

There was no point in discussing it. Ruel blamed himself for this. He should have stayed with them up there instead of running out on the party.

"Let's get some sleep," he said. But it was Woody who did the sleeping. Ruel tossed and turned, and didn't get to sleep until morning.

13

Ruel woke up at noon, feeling ragged, ashamed of having slept through the best part of the day. Woody's bunk was unoccupied. After pulling into his clothes and washing up at the well pump, Ruel walked across to the house.

He found Jean scrubbing a kitchen floor which was already, as he could see, spotless.

"Dad's in town," she said, in response to Ruel's question. "I'm worried about him, Ruel. He rode out two times this morning to see if there was any water in the creek. I've never seen him in such a temper. There's no telling what he'll do if he runs into Frank Gant."

"Did Woody go into town with him?"

She shook her head. "Woody's out on the range."

"Maybe I'd better mosey on into Chenango."

"You'd be taking your life in your hands, Ruel," said Jean, and a shadow seemed to fall on her. "I've heard about last night."

"How can I help then?"

"I could use some advice."

"Advice?"

She told him about Woody's offer. "It's a temptation, Ruel. I can't imagine why Frank Gant wants C Bar, but after what happened last night I wouldn't put anything past him. Dad said this morning that he should have hanged Frank." Her own words made her shudder. "Ruel, I'm scared. I have a feeling something horrible is going to happen. Woody's offer *is* a way out."

"It is," Ruel said, "provided your father would accept it. Have you spoken to him about it?"

Jean shook her head.

"Why not?"

Jean hesitated. It seemed to Ruel that her cheeks were unnaturally red. "I think this is Woody's way of telling me he wants to marry me."

"Oh?" Suddenly he couldn't look at her. He had that empty ache in his chest.

"He hasn't come right out and said so. I'm almost sure that's what's in his mind though." Jean's smile was rueful. "It's not a very romantic way for a girl to be proposed to, is it?"

"What's the problem?" Ruel asked, trying to keep this on an impersonal level.

"What do you think I ought to do?" In her eyes he saw a wistfulness, a question. "I don't want anyone to be hurt."

Ruel thought, You think I'm not hurting? He said, "This is something you're going to have to work out for yourself, Jean. It's between you and your conscience."

"Yes," she said. "Yes." And then, that wistfulness in her eyes: "Where will you be, Ruel, when all this has blown over? Will you stay in the basin?"

"Not likely," Ruel murmured.

"What will you do? Where will you go?"

"I'll be on the move, somewhere."

"You like that, don't you? Being on the move?"

"It isn't always a question of what you like in this life." The blue eyes looked into his, puzzled, but he had said all he intended to say on that subject. Jean, sensing it, rose, and turned toward her stove.

It was a pleasure to watch her move around C Bar's kitchen as she prepared a lunch for him. With a place for everything, and everything in its place, she got things done quickly and efficiently without seeming to hurry.

The heat of the stove heightened her color. A wisp of hair kept falling down over her forehead; she pushed it away with the back of her hand. For some reason Ruel found that gesture profoundly affecting. He wanted to leave his place at the oil-clothed table and take her in his arms.

Remembering the night he had kissed her, sitting on the bunkhouse steps, and how she'd responded before pulling away, Ruel thought, Why'd she tell me that about Woody? So I'd know where she stands with him? Maybe she likes me.

But that was too much to hope for. He refused to think about it.

He went outside, after he'd eaten, and cut some wood for Jean's stove—as good a way as any, he thought as he brought the ax whipping down, to work off tensions.

Lucas, on his return from Chenango, had a faraway look in his eyes. He was strangely quiet at the dinner table. Jean tried to draw him out, but Lucas replied to her questions in monosyllables.

Later that night in the bunkhouse, Woody commented on it to Ruel. "What's botherin' Lucas? What'd he want in town?"

"I wouldn't know," Ruel said.

"You ask me, he's up to somethin'." It didn't worry Woody too much. Within a few minutes he had turned in and was snoring.

Ruel stared at a shifting shadow pattern on the wall across from the window. He couldn't get his mind off the girl, and what she'd said to him. He asked himself again and again if her interest in him might be more than friendly.

Finally he gave up trying to sleep, and went outside for a smoke and a look at the night. He was perched on a willow stump down by the horse pasture when he saw Lucas Wright come tiptoeing out of the house carrying his boots.

Lucas, after pulling his boots on, walked across the yard toward the corral. He opened the gate just enough to ease his way into the enclosure. He emerged, presently, leading his blanketed horse, his saddle slung over one down-tilted shoulder. He didn't saddle up until he'd walked his horse away from the buildings.

He rode off into the night, finally, without having ventured one glance in Ruel's direction.

Ruel snaked his own horse out of the corral and followed the older man out onto the moonlit grass flat. Lucas, he saw, had reined in alongside the huge live oak tree that was C Bar's most prominent landmark, and was

105

talking to Yancey Jefford, who apparently had been waiting there for him.

Ruel rode over to the pair and gave them a dry, "Howdy?"

"Don't you sleep?" asked Lucas aggrievedly.

"I couldn't, tonight. What's goin' on?" Lucas didn't answer, and Ruel said, "You boys didn't ride out here in the dead of the night to play checkers. What're you up to?"

"That'd be our business, wouldn't it, son?" Yancey Jefford asked mildly.

Lucas had something in his hand, and was trying to hide it behind his body.

"What've you got there?" Ruel asked him.

"Where?"

"In your left hand."

Lucas sighed. "Your eyes are too sharp, man."

Ruel said, "That wouldn't by any chance be dynamite, would it?"

Lucas said wryly, "Would it do me any good to deny it?"

"Are you thinking of blowing that dam, Lucas?" Ruel asked.

Lucas was silent. Yancey spoke for him. "That's right. And I aim to help him."

"How do you come into this?" Ruel asked.

"Well now, I'll tell you. Happens I was in Chenango last Wednesday, and who comes along but Frank Gant and that professional killer he's put on his payroll."

"You mean McLouth?" Ruel asked.

The tall, stoop-shouldered man nodded. "They tried to crowd me off the walk into the gutter. I wasn't having any of that. I gave a pretty fair account of myself for the first couple minutes. Then they called in reinforcements. I got the same medicine you got from Frank Gant, son, your first day in this country."

Ruel could understand, now, why Lucas had been so uncommunicative on his return from town. He said, "You mean Y Lightning ganged up on you there in town, and nobody helped you?"

"Mart Gilman tried."

"Gilman?"

"He runs the only decent saloon in town, son. He'd just stepped out of his place, on some errand or other. He made a grab at Frank's arm. He got kind of green around the gills and backed off when Frank cussed him out and threatened to shoot him. I wasn't wearin' my gun or I'd've used it on Frank then. . . . Jenny don't let me wear a gun in town."

"Seems to me *some*body could've done something."

"Son, you got to bear in mind that Frank's crew was in there. Chenango ain't the same since Con Wishard turned in his badge and left us without any law enforcement. Frank's got this range buffaloed." The older man sighed. "I never brought you up-to-date on Mart, did I, Lucas? He's leavin' town, soon as he can find a buyer for his place."

"The hell he is?"

"It don't sound like him, does it? It's too bad. I understand some of the others are talkin' of pullin' up stakes too." Yancey Jefford turned toward Ruel. "If somebody don't soon throw a fall into Frank he'll wind up ownin' this whole range by default."

They were all silent, sobered by Yancey's statement. Lucas said finally, "How'd you leave Jenny? Does she know you're here? Or did you sneak out, same as I did?"

"Hell, no," Yancey said. "I just got up when the time come and put my clothes on and skedaddled."

"You mean to say," Lucas said wonderingly, "Jenny give you permission to ride out here?"

"As a matter of fact, she raised hell." Yancey paused. There was self-conscious pride in his voice as he added, "Way I look at it, this is as much my fight as yours. I told her this was somethin' I had to do, and that was all there was to it. She was sputterin' at me hard and heavy when I walked out. I closed my ears to it and kept on walkin'. There comes a time in a man's life when he's got to declare himself."

"Do tell," Lucas said. "I was wonderin' when you'd realize it. Congratulations."

Ruel had been thinking, as these older men talked, about what they intended to do.

"You can't blow that dam, Lucas," he said.

"Why can't I?"

"You'd never get anywhere near it. You'd never get past the guard."

"I'm still goin' to try. I've got to try, damn it."

"Why have you?"

There was an awkward silence. Lucas sighed, and said reluctantly, "You two may's well know this. The bank's holding more of my paper than I like to think about. All I've got in the world is my equity in C Bar, and that sure ain't much. If I sold out to Frank for what's offered I wouldn't have nothing left after payin' my debts."

Ruel whistled softly. He had suspected this. It still was a shock, hearing Lucas spell it out in so many words.

"There's no point in you and Yancey riding out to that dam, Lucas," Ruel said.

"I think there is."

"You want to get yourself shot? Think of Jean, if you won't think of yourself."

"She'll be all right. She told me tonight about a proposition Woody's come up with. Seems like he's salted some money away and—"

"I know. She told me about that."

"Woody's all right. He's dependable, and he'll work hard to make my girl happy. 'Course I can't accept that partnership offer. If I'm squeezed off C Bar I won't have a dime in my pocket. I'd make him a hell of a partner. I won't live with them, either. Young people starting out don't want their folks around."

"Where would you go, Lucas? What would you do?"

"I don't know. I just don't know," Lucas said. He looked up. "You see now why I figure I've got to blow that dam?"

Ruel stared out across the dark prairie, mulling over Lucas's problem. "I can see how you feel," he said at last. He straightened in the saddle. "Shall we get goin'?"

"Who rung you in on this?" Lucas asked.

"I'll ride along," Ruel said, pleasantly.

"This ain't your party."

You're right, Lucas, he thought. It isn't my party. But I'll ride along.

The older man, apparently sensing it was useless to argue, sighed and touched his horse with his boot heels.

They rode for some minutes in silence, infected by the chill of the night and by the thought of their mission. This is goin' to be bad, Ruel thought. Frank's probably doubled the guard at the dam. How're we supposed to get close enough to it to blow it? Why am I here anyway? I must be gettin' soft-headed.

These oldtimers have what it takes, though. When they're hit, they hit back. This range'd be better off if there were more like them around here.

So she's goin' to marry Woody. Well, why not? As Lucas says, she could do worse. She's not for me. She never was. I guess I always knew it.

They crossed a lowland with a cold wind buffeting them, their horses making little sound on the dry, chalky earth. The ridge of C Bar's mountain stood out murkily, silhouetted against the sky northward, providing a landmark.

They passed a rock cairn, a boundary marker for Y Lightning's far-flung holdings. They were in enemy territory now; they rode with caution.

When they had come within half a mile of the dam, Lucas drew rein.

"This ought to do it," he said.

Ruel could see Y Lightning's fire—a point of brightness against the blue-black horizon ahead. He caught the glimmer of moonlight on the mirror surface of the reservoir Frank's dam had created.

"How you figuring to go about this, Lucas?"

Lucas was holding that stick of dynamite in his hand as he answered. "S'pose I leave my horse here with you, and work my way in on foot."

Ruel winced. "Lucas, the only way you'll get within a stone's throw of that dam is by crawlin' in on your belly. Even so, you'd never make it from this side."

"Why not?"

"The moon's behind us, you'll notice. So's the wind. One of their horses would pick up your scent."

"I'll go in from the other side then."

"No," said Ruel quietly. "I will."

"Now hold on a damn minute. If you think I'm goin' to let you take—"

"I'm the man for this," Ruel said.

Lucas, plainly unconvinced of it, snorted.

"You askin' for my credentials?" Ruel murmured.

"Credentials?" He could feel the older man peering owlishly at him.

"Maybe I'd better tell you who I am, Lucas."

"I don't just follow you, son. What's that supposed to mean?"

14

Ruel sat there an instant. "I guess you've heard of Dude Maxon."

Lucas shook his head. "Who's he?"

"He was my father."

Yancey Jefford said confusedly, "But—your name's Matheson, ain't it?"

"Pop changed his name pretty often. The one he used most was Maxon. He used to run with Stan Lee Pecos and Bignose George Roth and Billy Kid Vardon up around Sheridan, Wyoming. You must've heard of them."

"Can't say as I have," Lucas said.

"I've heard of them," put in Yancey. "They made quite a name for themselves robbin' trains and holdin' up banks, and I don't know what all else, about fifteen years ago."

"Pop was with them less than a year," Ruel said. "He got shot durin' a holdup, and rode off into the hills alone to false-trail the posse. He was near dead by the time they caught up with him. He shot one posseman dead and winged another. They—they strung him up from a railroad trestle."

"Son, if I'd known you had anything like that weighin' on your mind I wouldn't've asked you to help me string Frank up. This father of yours sounds like one hell of a man."

"Pop was all right. He was part Indian. People wouldn't let him forget it, and he turned mean. I was thirteen when they hanged him. The gang tried to raise me. Bignose taught me to throw a knife, and to move around in the dark without making a sound. The Kid spent his spare time teachin' me to use a gun. Before I was out of my teens I could get my gun into action faster than he could, and

111

still hit what I aimed at. And he was the fastest draw in the gang."

"So *that's* how come that rattler lost his head," murmured Lucas. "Woody told me what a near thing you had up on the ledge, son."

"I broke away from the gang when I came of age," Ruel said. "I signed on as wrangler with a trail drive. When the drive got to Abilene the fellow that owned the herd—he was one of those damn fools who didn't believe in banks—delivered the herd to a buyer and took payment in cash. He strapped eight thousand dollars around his waist in a money belt and got drunk as a skunk—so naturally somebody rolled him. My past was known. When part of the money was found in my bedding out at camp, I was a dead pigeon."

Lucas clucked sympathetically. "How many years did they send you up for, son?"

"Five." Ruel couldn't keep the bitterness out of his voice. "I served four years, three months, and twenty-seven days of that sentence, and all I've got to show for it is a pretty fair game of checkers."

"Better'n that," Lucas said.

Yancey said, "I take it they let you off for good behavior?"

Ruel laughed shortly. "Nothin' like it."

"Then—"

"I saw my chance and broke out."

The two older men held to an uneasy silence.

"You sure that was wise?" Lucas asked. "With less than a year to go?"

"All I know is I'm out," Ruel said, "and glad of it."

"You'd be some gladder, wouldn't you, if you'd served out your time and was really free? How old are you, Ruel?"

"Twenty-eight. Why?"

"You could serve the rest of your time and be out again, with a clean slate, before you reach thirty."

"I'm not doing any more time for a crime I never committed."

Ruel heard Lucas sigh. "What d' you want out of life, son? What d' you see in your future?"

112

"Not another year or two in Kitannining."

"Not a little place of your own? A wife, and maybe a couple of kids?"

"I'm not interested in those things."

"Why ain't you?"

"I guess I'm kind of a lone wolf."

Lucas snorted. "Ruel, I spent most of my life behind a store counter. There ain't no better place to observe human nature. If you're sayin' the matin' instinct's been trained out of you, I say hogwash. I just don't believe it."

"You think any nice girl'd want to marry me, have children by me?" Ruel asked.

"Why in hell not?" Ruel didn't reply, and the older man said, "If you're worried about bein' part Injun, forget it. A little cross-breedin' gen'rally upgrades the stock. Ain't that a fact, Yancey?"

"Hell, yes. I'm part Injun myself," said Yancey Jefford.

"My father was hanged for an outlaw," Ruel said. "My mother worked in a—in a saloon."

"What of it?" Lucas said. "This here's the west, man. Out here you're judged by what you are, not by your past, or your family connections."

Ruel felt encouraged to say, after a moment, "You think I did wrong to break out of jail?"

"How long ago'd you make the break, son?"

"Three years."

"How've you enjoyed those three years?"

Ruel shrugged. "I've got around some. I've seen the other side of a few hills."

"So did I, when I was your age. I got around, as you call it, just enough to satisfy myself what's over one hill ain't much different from what's over another. If I was you, I'd go back and finish my time out."

"I was framed," Ruel said. "I never took a damned cent of that money."

"All right, I believe you. But let me ask you this, son. While you was running with the gang did you do anything you ain't proud of? Anything, let's say, that you could of been sent up for?"

"Sure," Ruel said. "I was a full-fledged, working member of the gang for two years. But that's not the point.

The point is I was sent up for a job I had nothing to do with."

"What about the jobs you did have somethin' to do with?"

"What about them?"

Lucas was pointedly silent.

Ruel said, "I *had* to take part in those jobs, Lucas. As a member of the gang I—"

"Let's see, how old did you say you was when you run off?" Lucas asked.

"I was twenty-one," Ruel said.

"Seems to me, if you had a mind to, you might've made the break sooner."

"If I had, and they'd caught me at it, they'd've whaled me," Ruel said.

"You ask me, they gave you somethin' a damn sight worse'n a whalin'. They gave you their viewpoint. You seem to think you don't have to trouble your mind about any of those jobs you helped them pull off, because you never got caught. That's like sayin' the only crime is gettin' caught."

Something twisted and turned inside Ruel.

Lucas said, "Ruel, you had that stretch comin'. There ain't but one way to get right with yourself now."

"Don't tell me to go back to jail. Because I'm not goin'."

There was a long silence.

"Look," Ruel said, "I only brought this up to convince you I'm the man for this job."

"Why should you carry wood to our fire?" Lucas asked.

"Because I can get the job done. And I'm not sure you can."

"That's pretty blunt, son."

"No time for weasel words." Realizing that he had hurt the older man's pride, Ruel went on quickly: "I'll need your help to give them the slip, once the job's done."

"Oh?"

"What can we do?" asked Yancey.

"Slide in as close as you can. When the dam goes, start shagging some lead past their ears."

"You ain't askin' much of us," Lucas grumbled. After

114

thinking about it a moment, he handed the dynamite to Ruel. "We'll give 'em something to think about while you're getting away. On one condition."

"What's that?"

"Promise me you'll back away from this thing, if it looks too chancey."

"All right," Ruel said. "And if I were you two I wouldn't hang around to admire the moon, once the job's done."

"I expect we'll have business elsewhere," said Yancey drily.

Lucas grasped Ruel by the hand. "Luck, son," he said, his voice husking.

Ruel rode back the way they had come, turning slowly northward and westward. He got his legs wet fording the Whitewoman upstream from the dam. He rode on in gray discomfort.

Why'd I take this job on? How'm I going to get anywhere near that dam?

There was nothing to keep him from riding out. All he had to do was pull the dun around and put the spurs to him. Well, why not? What am I hangin' around for? She doesn't care anything about me. She's as good as promised herself to Woody Yarmon.

He ground his teeth in self-contempt and pushed on, veering more to his left now. Five miles of steady riding brought him full about; he had Y Lightning's fire and the moon in front of him, and was riding into the teeth of the wind.

Now if only he could be sure of the wind, sure that it would not change direction.

His feet were numb, swollen in his wet boots. He tethered his horse to a skinny mesquite, and moved in toward Y Lightning's fire on his hands and knees.

The sky overhead was partly obscured by cirrus. Only the two bright stars of Orion, blue-white Rigel and red Betelgeuse, shone through the veil-like clouds, standing out like a pair of diamonds.

A coyote yelped in the distance. It was hard not to envy the animal's freedom. Lucky Mr. Coyote. You've got no conscience tellin' you what to do. You're free to run where your fancy takes you.

When he had come within a quarter mile of Y Lightning's camp he dropped down into the stream bed. The creek here below the dam was dry except for a trickle of water meandering along its sand-and-gravel bottom. Ruel pushed on, hugging moon shadow beneath the cutbanks, taking more care with his footing. He wound up wriggling along in a prone position, moving an inch or two at a time, pausing repeatedly to assure himself he had not alerted the men at the fire.

When he had come within ten yards of the dam, with Y Lightning's camp on the creek bank above him, he heard one of them say, on a note of complaint: "Christ Jesus, it's cold."

"What's the matter?" a second voice murmured.

"All I got to say is if Frank don't pull me off this detail I'm gonna ride in and ask for my time."

"You do, and you'll catch hell for leavin' your post."

"Not if I ain't workin' for the outfit, I won't."

"What's eatin' you, Cass?"

"I'm fed up, that's all. How long we been here, eight days goin' on nine? That's too long to keep a man on this kind of a detail. Frank ought to rotate us more often."

"He ought to. He ain't about to, so let's make the best of it."

"Not me. When I'm horsed around, I figure to raise hell about it."

"Relax, Cass. We're bein' paid to sit here and do nothin', in case you're forgettin'."

"What's the use havin' money in your pocket, if you can't spend it?"

"We'll get into town. Our turn'll come."

"What's he need six men here for?" Cass said. "Nobody's come near the dam, much less tampered with it. Four'd be plenty."

"Frank don't see it that way."

"Don't he? That's too bad how he don't see it."

"He's the boss. He gives the orders."

"The hell with his orders."

"Look, you're gettin' yourself all lathered up, and what good'll it do you? You want to work off some steam, rustle some wood for the fire."

"Not me. I rustled the last load."

"You're in a fine frame of mind, ain't you?"

Ruel heard the man named Cass grunt and move away from the fire. He appeared suddenly up above on the creek bank, silhouetted against the night sky, seemingly larger than life, and Ruel could feel his heart pounding. He lay not moving, not breathing as the moon's glow strengthened and this night became, as it seemed to him, bright as day. His neck itched, and he didn't dare scratch it. He cut off a compulsive desire to sneeze by pressing a finger against his upper lip.

His eyes never left the man on the bank. He sees me. He must. He's just not letting on. He's playing cat and mouse with me, damn him.

The man bent, to pick up a pebble, and tossed it, with an underhand motion, down into the creek bed. It struck an imbedded stone near Ruel's head, bounced and rolled clattering to a stop. Ruel didn't move. The man above turned back toward the fire.

"What was that?" his companion asked him.

"What?"

"What was you up to over there by the crick, Cass? You chuck somethin' down in there?"

"That's right."

"Why'd you do that?"

"I thought I seen a man layin' down in there."

"A man?"

"It wasn't nothin'. Just one of them tricky moon shadows."

"You sure? Let's have a look."

"It ain't nothing. It ain't worth bothering about," Cass said.

"Thing like that's always worth bothering about," said the other. "Come on." Both of them appeared on the bank above Ruel. "Where'd you see this moon shadow?"

"There."

It was all Ruel could do to lie still. Only the presence of

that dynamite in his hand, reminding him why he had come here, prevented him from whipping his gun out.

"Where?"

"Right there." The man named Cass picked up another pebble and threw it at Ruel.

15

Ruel, struck on the boot, still did not move. The men above went on talking.

"Does look like a man, kind of. Slide down there and have a look, why don't you, Cass?"

"Not me."

"What's the matter?"

"I ain't goin' down there. You could easy as not sprain your ankle, a dark night like this."

"That's all that's worryin' you, is it?" laughed the first man. "Well, there's a way to find out if our imagination's playin' tricks on us. Put a bullet into that shadow."

Ruel could feel the hammer strike of his pulse. Do something. Don't stay here and make a sitting duck target for them. Cut them down, and run for it. It's your only chance now.

His fingers tightened around the stick of dynamite in his hand. He held his breath as one of the men above said, "Go ahead, Cass."

"Go ahead where?"

"I'm gettin' cold away from the fire. You goin' to shoot, or ain't you?"

"I dunno as I ought to."

"What's the matter?"

"That ain't no man. A man would've moved by now."

"Only one way to be sure."

"I ain't going to shoot. There's four men sawin' wood over there by the fire. They'll raise hell if I wake them up."

"Let them. Go ahead, shoot."

"It's easy for you to say go ahead, shoot. You ain't the one they'll raise hell with." Cass walked away. His companion lingered a moment, then he, too, returned to the comfort and warmth of the fire.

Ruel scratched his neck, and permitted himself the luxury of drawing a normal breath. He felt strangely tired, as though he'd done a day's work in the past several minutes. He was cold to the marrow.

He rubbed up circulation in his legs and arms. Still carrying the dynamite in his left hand, he inched forward.

It took him fifteen minutes to work his way to the base of the dam, a crude affair made of brush and mud backed up against a framework of logs lashed together with rawhide. There was no way to avoid exposing himself, while he was placing the charge.

What was it Lucas had said? "Back off, if it looks too chancey." Ruel shook his head, annoyed at the turn his thoughts had taken. He drew a long breath. Working with careful precision, he slid the dynamite into a hole in the dam that was big enough, he found, to accommodate his arm. Drawing a match from a weatherproof tin in his pocket, he scraped it across the edge of his boot heel.

It failed to ignite. As he was debating where else to strike it, a voice spoke out of the darkness above him: "What was that?"

"What?"

"That sound."

"What sound? I never heard nothing."

"Kind of a scratching sound. Sounded to me like it come from over there in the crick bed."

"Well, have a look. Don't stand here jawin' about it."

Ruel swore. Moving with desperate haste, he struck his match on the butt of his gun and cupped its flame to the fuse. As the sputtering asterisk marched along the fuse toward the charge, he ran back along the creek bottom, holding his gun against his leg to keep it from chafing.

Behind him one of Frank Gant's guards shouted, "Who's there?"

Another voice, hoarse with excitement, said, "Plug him, Cass. Plug him. He's tryin' to blow the dam."

Guns crashed behind Ruel. He ran faster. The darkness and the unfamiliar, uneven footing were a double handicap to him. His foot skidded off an eroded smooth stone. He fell headlong.

A slug whipped past his head like an angry wasp. He would have been knocked down by that bullet, if he had not fallen. Keep moving, he thought. You'll drown like a rat down here in the crick bed if you don't keep moving.

The enemy camp was aroused, after him in full force now. Lead came at him in a fusillade. He was hit in the leg as he tried to climb the creek bank. He grasped the root of an undercut tree, and hauled himself up onto high ground.

Lucas and Yancey, out on the grass, were laying down the barrage they had promised. The men across the creek were forced to take cover. One of them slithered down into the creek bed, and ran toward the dam.

"Come back, you damn fool. That thing's ready to blow!" The man Cass, ignoring the warning, tried to pinch out the flame in the fuse between his thumb and forefinger. He burnt himself and let go.

There was a blinding flash, a *whomp* of explosion as the charge ignited. The ground under Ruel shook and trembled. The dam seemed to rise up and spread out like a fast-growing mushroom. Water piled through a gaping hole in a relentless tide that carried everything, including Cass, with it.

Ruel felt a shuddering weakness inside. A few minutes ago that poor devil had complained about being mistreated and threatened to ask for his time. What in God's name had possessed the fellow? He had not seemed the sort that heroes are made of. There was a gruesome irony in the way he had died.

Across the creek, one of the men yelled, "By God, he's killed Cass. Nail the bastard!"

Ruel wriggled along, hugging the ground. A bullet tugged at his brush-popper jacket, and he winced, feeling his flesh draw in on itself. He lay still for a moment, trying to quiet his ragged breathing.

With the tips of his fingers he explored the wound in his leg, which had already bloodied his Levis. Better get a bandage on that, he thought, as he eased himself down into a shallow dry ditch.

He wrapped his bandanna around the leg, but he had trouble tying it in place with his cold, trembling fingers. He retched and gagged at the taste of bile in his throat.

It occurred to him that Frank Gant's men could not cross the creek until the water released by the blowing of the dam subsided. To get at him quickly they would have to seek a ford somewhere upstream. Lucas and Yancey were still popping away from out on the grass.

Ruel heard a voice say, "Couple of you Injun out there and put a stop to that."

"What about our friend across the crick, Hurd?"

"Don't worry about him. He won't get far. I got a feelin' we pulled his stopper with one of them bullets."

"You mean—"

"Somethin' tells me he ain't in no shape to sit a horse."

Think again, friend. I'm not as bad off as that. Ruel crawled along the gully, favoring the hurt leg. When he had gone ten yards he stopped, and thought about what he was doing. Cupping his hands to his mouth, he shouted, "Lucas, they're layin' for you. Line out. On the double."

He was rewarded, presently, by a clatter of hooves as Lucas and Yancey, acting on his suggestion, rode out.

Across the creek an angry voice said, "Let's go, boys."

"Where to, Hurd?"

"That's Matheson across the crick. Get your horses."

Ruel had heard enough to realize what he was in for. He dragged himself out along the gully, across the flat to his horse, and lifted himself painfully to the saddle.

He pulled in, after fifteen minutes of riding, and he could hear Frank Gant's men coming after him at a run. He had killed one of their number back at the dam, and made them look like incompetent fools in the process. He had no illusions as to what would happen to him when they overtook him.

He could feel blood oozing out of the bullet hole in his leg, beneath the inadequate bandage. It was an effort now to keep his place in the saddle. The dun horse, crossing uneven ground, broke stride. Ruel, thrown back against the high cantle of his Hamley saddle, groaned, and set his teeth against the throbbing misery in his leg.

He rode on, trying to ignore the leg, growing weaker by the minute.

I could use some of Jean's nursin', he thought. But damned if I'll run whimperin' to C Bar and pull a hornet's nest down on her head now.

He grasped the horn, straightening up in the saddle, and touched spurs to the dun.

16

Woody Yarmon sat up in his bunk, holding his blankets around him. He knuckled an eye, wondering grumpily what had aroused him. A murky, pre-dawn light streamed in the bunkhouse window. Ruel Matheson's bunk, he saw, was empty.

He heard voices and the muted tinkling of a bit-chain outside. Pulling into his clothes, he crossed to the window and saw that, while he slept, Frank Gant and a dozen of his Y Lightning crewmen had come riding into C Bar's tiny yard.

Lucas Wright stood in the doorway of the log house, a carbine propped in the crook of his arm. He had the disgruntled air of a man whose sleep has been interrupted.

"Kind of short-memoried, ain't you?" he growled at Frank. He stepped out of the doorway onto the gallery of the house. "You been told to stay off C Bar."

"Where's Matheson?" Frank asked.

"Why?"

"When he blew the dam he blew one of my men to hell-and-gone," Frank said. "I want him."

Frank's tone of voice as he said, "I want him," gave Woody the shivers. Woody strapped his gun around his waist somewhat reluctantly, and went out there. Frank's men turned their heads his way, taking note of his presence. Frank nodded at him in a negligent way, then ignored him.

"Where's Matheson, Lucas?"

Jean had come out of the house to stand by her father. Lucas, Woody saw, drew strength from her presence. The old man gave Frank a flat stare.

"You got any bone to pick for what's happened, you can pick it with me."

"I want that drifter," Frank said. Woody could see that the big man was losing patience with Lucas. "Where is he? In the house?"

Lucas and the girl exchanged glances. They faced Frank in silent defiance. Frank had the look of a frustrated animal as he spoke to his men. "Climb down, boys. We'll see for ourselves if he's here."

"You ain't searchin' my house," Lucas said.

Frank's crooked smile made his handsome face almost ugly. He and two of his men climbed off their horses and walked toward the house. Lucas moved over, placing himself in their way.

"Stand aside," Frank said, and that was when Lucas brought up the carbine and pointed it at Frank's chest.

Frank ground to a halt. He stared at the carbine, and at the determined face of the middle-aged man aiming it at him.

"Put that away, Lucas."

Lucas, Woody saw, was rigid with anger. "Stand back," he said, "or by God, I'll let you have it."

Frank eyed him a curious instant, then turned to the girl.

"Talk to him."

She looked at him as if he were some kind of reptile. Frank moved one leg tentatively forward. Lucas said, "You think I won't pull this trigger?"

Frank, Woody saw with surprise, was smiling again in his toothy way.

"You do, Lucas," he said, "and you'll be dead in a hurry. You and your hand over there by the bunkhouse. Maybe even the girl."

"You wouldn't do anything to her," said Lucas.

"*I* wouldn't," Frank said. "I can't speak for my boys, though. They're kind of quick on the trigger. One of them might go berserk and start sprayin' lead around here if you cut me down."

Lucas, tormented by doubt, appeared to sag and grow old as he faced the still-smiling Y Lightning owner.

Jean said, "He's bluffing, Dad. Don't listen to him. He was a gambler, remember."

Lucas had made his decision.

"Have a look," he said to Frank. "Then get out of here and stay out of here, damn it."

Frank waved his men toward the open door. They went into the house cautiously, flattening themselves against the jamb. They came out after two minutes, wagging their heads.

"He ain't in there."

"Hurd," Frank said, "you and Coley give those buildings a look-see. Quick now," he growled, as they hesitated.

When they came back to report having found no sign of the drifter, Frank snarled at Lucas, "Where is he?"

"You think if I knew I'd tell you?" asked Lucas.

"We'll get him," Frank said. "It'll be all over for him when we do."

"You've got no quarrel with Ruel," Lucas said. His manner was less truculent now, Woody noticed.

"If it wasn't for him—" Frank shook his head "—you and I'd've done business by now. We'll have a talk after he's taken care of."

"Will we?"

"Make up your mind to it." Frank, as he climbed onto his roan stallion, kept one eye on Lucas. He didn't relax, Woody noticed, until he and his men had ridden out of the yard.

Lucas propped the carbine against the building and put an arm around Jean, who was trembling. She's had a scare for herself, Woody thought. Never let on till they left though. That's courage—bein' scared and refusin' to show it.

They went in the house. While Jean made coffee, Lucas told Woody what had happened during the night.

"Ruel convinced me he was the man for that job," Lucas said ruefully. "I s'pose he was right. Nobody else could've got near that dam, much less dynamite it. He's mixed up pretty bad though."

"Mixed up," said Jean. "How Dad?"

"He's got some ideas he could do without, honey."

"What kind of ideas?" Jean asked as she poured coffee. Lucas curled his fingers around the mug, drawing

126

warmth from it. "He needs to think better of himself. If he straightens his thinking out, he'll make some pretty little trick a fine husband."

Jean's color heightened and Woody, watching her, thought, What's goin' on here?

"Where do you suppose he is, Dad?"

"Wish I knew." Lucas sighed. "I got a hunch he was hit."

"Wouldn't he come here if he was?"

"He might. On the other hand, he might not," Lucas said.

"But if he's hurt and needs help—you—you don't suppose he could be dead?" Jean's eyes were sick at the thought.

"Honey," Lucas said, "I don't know. I just don't know."

"If he's been hit they'll find him, won't they? They'll track him down, now that it's light." She put her hands over her face and lowered her head. It was all she could do to hold the tears back. Woody's sympathy for her was tainted by envy of the man whose welfare so greatly concerned her.

Jean turned toward him now and said, "What do you think?"

"For all we know," Woody said, "he could be out of the basin by this time."

"That's not likely, is it?"

"Not if he was hit," Woody admitted. Jean rose unsteadily and went into her bedroom and closed the door. Woody could hear her crying softly inside there.

No man could hear that and not be affected. Woody and Lucas exchanged weary glances. Woody inclined his head toward Jean's door.

"Guess she figures we ought to be doin' somethin' for Ruel. But what can we do? We can't ride out and leave her alone here."

"Besides which," Lucas said bitterly, "I wouldn't know where to ride to. Who's to say where he's holed in? I hate to hear her carryin' on though."

"Me, too." Would she carry on like that if it was *me* Frank and his crew'd took out after? Woody wondered about that as he ate breakfast. Jean and her father ate hardly anything. Woody made a point of picking at his own food, although he was hungry enough to eat a horse. They hung around home buildings that morning. At lunch they sat moping, making occasional talk in an effort to get their minds off Ruel.

After lunch, Woody followed Lucas outside. "I may's well ride out," he said, trying to sound casual. "Just might be able to do somethin' for Ruel, if Frank hasn't got him already."

Lucas eyed him gravely. He gestured toward the house. "It's her you're thinkin' of, ain't it?"

Woody nodded.

"Could go hard on you," Lucas said, "if you run afoul of Frank and his outfit."

"I know."

"Sure you want to risk it?"

Woody hesitated, feeling coldness inside. Lucas was watching him, he knew. He said, "You s'pose Jean'd mind fixin' me some grub to take with me, while I'm catchin' my horse up?"

"Mind?" The older man clapped Woody affectionately on the back. "Don't talk so damn foolish," he said, in his husky voice.

When later Woody was about to climb on his horse and ride out, Jean stood on tiptoes and kissed him. He wore a foolish, self-conscious smile all the way out C Bar's lane. Then the thought came: She did that because she's worried sick about Ruel. He's the one she's interested in. The realization gave him an achey feeling inside. He tried not to think about it as he urged his horse up a rise.

He had a hunch where Ruel—if not too badly hurt to stay on a horse—might have headed for after dynamiting the dam.

He dropped down into an arroyo, and stayed with it for a mile, moving steadily northward. A jackrabbit, as Woody rounded a bend, sat and stared at him with one ear erect, one hanging limply, then, after a series of bewildering, zigzag jumps, shot forward and was gone from view. A jay screeched at him as he left the basin floor and moved up into the foothills. From somewhere to his right, within a dense thicket, came the *psee-eek* of a cowbird.

He had a feeling of hidden eyes focused on him. He reined in without warning and turned around in the saddle. He could see nothing out of the ordinary behind him, nothing to indicate that he was being followed. As he left the foothills, he reined around for another sharp scrutiny of his back trail.

I'm actin' like an old woman, he thought. He urged his horse on up the slope.

Some yards below the boulder field near which Ruel had found water, Woody's horse paused to nip at a tuft of grass. Woody, after debating a moment, tethered the animal to a dwarf piñon, and went on afoot, heading for the cavelike opening under the ledge that Ruel had identified as the handiwork of a Mexican shepherd.

He saw no sign of Ruel in the cave or anywhere near it. Woody paused in his climbing and sighed, wondering if he had guessed wrong.

"Ruel?"

After a long silence broken only by the twittering of birds in a thicket, Ruel spoke from behind a clutter of rocks twenty yards to the right of the cave.

"Who is it?" Ruel did not show himself. Woody heard the unmistakable click of a gun being cocked.

"Me. Woody."

"Who's with you?"

"Nobody."

Ruel thrust one eye, and no more of his head than he had to, out from behind a jagged edge of rock. Apparently what he saw reassured him; he exposed both eyes to Woody's view now.

"How'd you find me?"

Woody shrugged. "Lucas had a hunch you'd been hit. A hurt man'll generally hunt a hole to crawl into. I been thinking about you all morning, asking myself where I'd head for if I was in your fix. How come you're not in the cave?"

"I don't like bein' pinned down. It's got no rear exit."

Woody studied the blood-stained bandanna wrapped around Ruel's left leg above the knee. He shuddered.

"How bad is it?"

"I've lost some blood," said Ruel matter-of-factly. If I'd been through what he's been through the past four or five hours, Woody thought, I'd be wallowing in self-pity.

"Why didn't you head for C Bar after they put the hole in you, Ruel?"

"How's Lucas?" Ruel asked. "He get home all right, did he?"

Woody described the reception Lucas had given Frank Gant and his men when they rode into C Bar. "That old man came damn near shootin' Frank."

Ruel, grinning, half closed his eyes, then he sobered. "So now the hunt's on." He looked bone tired, but his eyes were bright, and somehow eager, as though the prospect of being run down and shot at gave him pleasure. It didn't seem natural to Woody.

"You got to get out of here, Ruel," he said uneasily after a moment.

"Have I?"

"Frank Gant's nothin' but a damn butcher. He's out to kill you. He and his men went from C Bar back to the dam, to pick up your sign. They'll track you down."

"Maybe they won't. I rode through water in the upper part of the crick for close to a mile, last night, while I was decidin' where to head for. I came out where cattle are in the habit of taking water. There's probably nothing left of the prints I made comin' out of the crick." Ruel glanced up as a thought occurred to him. "Any chance you were followed here?"

Woody, remembering his nervousness as he entered the foothills, felt a stab of concern. "I don't think so."

"What's that mean?" Ruel frowned. "Aren't you sure?"

Woody gave a little lift of his shoulders. "I'm sure," he said, more firmly than he had any right to. From his coat pocket he took one of the beef sandwiches Jean had fixed for him. "How's this look to you, Ruel?"

Ruel put his hand out, grinning. He ate the sandwich slowly—to prolong the pleasure? Or to get as much nourishment as he could from it? When he had finished, he pointed at a seam of black rock that extended along one wall of the cave.

"Lucas ever say anything to you about this?"

Woody shook his head. "Obsidian, ain't it?"

"That's what I took it for our first time up here," Ruel said. "I've done a little exploring this morning. I know now it's coal. This little old mountain's loaded with the stuff, Woody. You make anything of that, do you?"

"What should I make of it?"

"Did I hear Lucas say Frank Gant's father mined coal for a living somewhere back East? Maybe that's what he's after, why he wants C Bar." As he spoke, Ruel cocked his head, cupping one hand to an ear, lifting one finger of the other toward his pursed lips. Woody couldn't hear anything, but after a moment Ruel said sharply, "Where'd you leave your horse?"

"Downslope a couple hundred yards, tied to a piñon. Why?"

"Stay put." Ruel started down the slope at a run, favoring his bandaged leg, managing somehow, despite the handicap, to move silently, swiftly.

Woody stood paralyzed, unable to decide on a course of action. He had been told to stay put, and although Ruel had no authority over him, he found it hard not to follow orders. But damn it, he's hurt. It's my horse he's worried about. And here I'm lettin' him take the play away from me.

Woody clapped a hand to his gun and went charging after Ruel, who had rounded a stand of piñons and was out of sight now.

As he reached the trees, Woody pulled up behind an outcropping of weathered granite. He had made more racket coming down here than he should have. He pushed his hat back off his head onto his shoulders, letting it hang by the thong around his neck, and poked his head up.

Ruel Matheson lay belly-flat behind a small, moundlike rise that afforded him only the flimsiest cover. He rose as Woody watched, and ran with his limping strides toward the protection of a man-sized boulder.

Two men, farther down the slope, moved out from behind a tangle of brush. One of them, mounted on a big

131

bay, held the reins of the other's horse. The second man was leading Woody's white-stockinged sorrel.

The sorrel, always unpredictable around strangers, ran at the man without warning now and nipped him on the upper arm.

Even at this distance Woody could see the man's face go red with rage. The fellow whipped the sorrel about the eyes with the ends of the reins. Woody ran out from behind his outcrop and shouted, "Hey, you, that's my horse!"

Things happened with bewildering swiftness. The man Woody'd yelled at let go of the reins, drew his gun and sent a slug up at Woody, who fired back, twice, before it came to him that the range was too great for a pistol.

The man below holstered his gun and made a running leap onto his horse's back. His companion drew a carbine from a quiverlike saddle sling and, with a cool, thoughtful expression, levered a cartridge into firing position.

Woody took off as if catapulted, hurling himself in a long dive toward the outcrop he had deserted. The carbine had come up into train, was tracking him, he knew, and he had an instant in which to anticipate the smash of the bullet.

He saw Ruel Matheson bring his gun up, thumbcocking and triggering in one smooth, lightning-quick motion. The man with the carbine sagged, clutched convulsively at the horn, and fell off his horse. Already, Woody saw, Ruel had fan-cocked, was sending a second slug down the slope in an effort to wing the other man of the pair.

That one was leaning down, jockey fashion, over his horse's withers, going away fast. Not even a marksman of Ruel Matheson's caliber could hope to hit such a target.

Woody rose, wiping dirt off his Levis with the flat of a hand that refused to stop trembling, and walked down to Ruel. He stared at the sprawled out, motionless figure of the man who had tried and failed, thanks to Ruel, to pot him with the carbine. He had a dry, choked-up feeling in his throat. His heart was trying to hammer its way out of his chest.

"Thanks," he said.

Ruel acknowledged it with a careless lift of his shoulders. He inclined his head toward Woody's horse. "Will he stand, do you think, when we get down to him?"

"I think so."

"Get him. Let's get out of here," Ruel said.

Woody approached the sorrel, calling him gently by name, and caught hold of the reins. Ruel bent to examine a crease wound on the animal's gaskin. Already horseflies had gathered about the exposed, bleeding flesh. The sorrel's tail swished around at them.

As the sorrel turned its head and looked at him, Woody could have sworn he saw an accusing look in the animal's eyes. "I should've held my fire," he murmured.

"Pretty long range, from where you were." There was no censure in Ruel's voice. Here was a man, Woody saw, who had learned to make the best of his luck, good or bad.

He watched blood trickle down the sorrel's twitching, quivering leg. "Will he be able to carry me with that?"

Ruel's eyes came up to meet his. "He will for a while."

"And then?"

"Then he won't."

Woody said in a voice that wouldn't stay down where it belonged, "What's goin' to happen to us, Ruel?"

17

"Get hold of yourself, man."

"What're we in for?"

Ruel's shoulders lifted, fell. "Frank and his men probably heard those shots. My guess is they're on their way up the mountain. The one I missed would've brought the rest of them back anyway. No matter how you slice it, it adds up to trouble."

Woody tried to swallow; his throat was so dry that he couldn't. "I been a help to you, I have," he choked out. "I steered them onto you, and then spoiled your play. If I hadn't yelled at them like a fool, you could've nailed the pair of them."

Ruel had the look of a man whose thoughts are on other, more important matters. "Bring him up to where I left my horse," he indicated the sorrel. "Time we got going."

Woody let himself look at the man on the ground, who lay with his mouth open, one booted leg twisted under him, one arm curled over his head, as though he were waving to somebody. But he wasn't waving. Or moving. Or breathing. He looked awful damn dead. Woody wished he hadn't looked at him.

"What about this one's horse, Ruel?"

"What about him?"

"He ran off somewhere when the shootin' started. He might still be close by."

"He might," Ruel admitted. "But we haven't got time to look for him. Or to stand here talkin' about him. Come on."

Ruel's horse was picketed up slope, on a little patch

of salt grass surrounded by trees. Woody held the dun while Ruel dragged himself into the saddle.

They rode straight up-mountain, pausing occasionally to let the horses blow. During one pause Ruel stared down fixedly at the foothills, and his long face grew longer.

"What's wrong?" Woody said. "What's the matter?"

"They heard us shootin' all right."

"How can you tell?"

Ruel pointed. "See that dead green patch in the trees? Near the lodgepole pine with the crow perchin' on it."

"What about it?"

"Keep your eye on it."

Almost as Ruel spoke, a dozen small birds, sparrows, Woody guessed, though he couldn't be sure at this distance, came skittering out of the trees. The crow atop the lodgepole gave a tentative flap of his wings, as if testing them. He took off, cawing shrilly, and came flying up mountain.

"Christ," Woody said, "let's get goin'. They'll be here before—"

"Take it easy." Ruel nodded down at the horses, both of which were breathing hard. "We'll go in a minute."

Woody waited with a rising impatience. Goddamnit, that's Frank Gant and his Y Lightning wolf pack down there, hot on our scent. Why let them close the gap on us? Ruel, he saw, had gone limp in the saddle, and was making the most of this respite. How in hell can he relax at a time like this? Woody wondered.

"How long you aimin' to sit here?"

Ruel roused himself. His head inclined toward the sorrel. "How's he makin' it?"

The sorrel had begun to limp very slightly, but you'd have to be riding him to detect it. Woody hesitated an instant, then laid his hand on the animal's slick, sweat-glistening neck. "He's all right. He's fine. For Christ's sake, let's go."

They went on up the mountain, Ruel leading the way. The timber thinned as they neared the crest. Woody had thought they would head down the other side, but Ruel rode along the exposed, flinty ridge.

"What's the idea?"

"Your horse is limping," Ruel said. "He'll last longer ridin' the ridge."

"They'll see us here," Woody grumbled. "Next thing we know they'll be shaggin' lead at us."

"Not for a while yet." Seeing the questioning look on Woody's face, Ruel explained, "They've got to climb the same mountain we climbed. And we had a start on them. We'll make better time up here on the flat than they'll make fighting the grade. Offhand, I'd say we've got half an hour's lead on them. If we keep our wits about us, that may be enough."

"Enough for what?"

Ruel indicated the late afternoon sun heeling over toward the horizon westward. "Be dark in a couple hours."

They rode along the ridge. Ruel, who was setting pace for them, seemed in no great hurry. After an hour Woody could have sworn he heard the Y Lightning men coming.

"For God's sake, let's move," he said. "They're closin' on us."

Ruel turned in the saddle. "We're giving them a run," he said in his quiet way.

"A *run*?" Woody said. "We're not running, we're walking."

"How's the sorrel holding up, Woody?"

"He's all right. He's fine. He—"

"He's limping more than he was," Ruel said.

Woody threw a harried glance over his shoulder. "The sorrel's all right," he insisted. "Still a lot of run in this fellow."

Ahead of them lay more of the ridge, a great stone saddle devoid of vegetation. Ruel said, "You figure to run him on that?"

"I'll chance it."

Ruel, indicating the lowering sun, said, "There's our chance," and went on at the same deliberate pace.

Woody kept glancing back over his shoulder. "Damn it, they're runnin' us down. You act like this was a picnic. Ain't you even scared?"

"I'm scared," Ruel said. "Plenty."

"When I'm scared," grumbled Woody, "I act scared."

"Fair enough," Ruel said. "I'll have to ask you to quit lookin' back though."

"Why?"

"Every time you hitch around in the saddle you throw your horse off his stride, just a little."

In a tactful way he had been dressed down. Woody supposed he deserved it. As they rode on he kept his eyes focused forward, and tried, by minor shifts of his weight in the saddle, to help the sorrel with his footing.

Ruel reined in at last and sat with his eyes half closed, listening for sound on their back trail. He turned off the ridge, down along the floor of a shallow gully and into a stand of evergreen trees. He pulled the dun around and sat waiting for Woody to join him.

"That'll be all for the sorrel."

"Whaddaya mean?" Woody patted the sorrel's glistening neck. "This horse isn't through yet."

"He flinches on every step. He's goin' lame in the shoulder. He couldn't carry you more than another half mile." Ruel, as he spoke, flicked his eyes about, studying the lay of the land here. "This'll do," he said.

"Do?" exclaimed Woody. "For what?"

"Take my horse," Ruel said. "We'll let the sorrel follow you on a lead rope. He won't be able to keep up with you for more than a couple of miles. But we'll keep our friends guessing."

Woody stood there, frowning intently.

"Why should I take your horse? I shot the sorrel. I'm responsible for—"

"That's not the idea."

"What *is* the idea?"

"Our friends are too close. It won't be dark for a while. What's needed now is a decoy. Turn the sorrel loose when you've gone two miles, and make a run for it. Give the dun his head, and he'll do the rest. He's got more bottom than you'd think, to look at him."

"What about you?"

"I'll manage."

"How, for hell's sake?" Woody said. "Hurt like you are, without a horse—"

"I've been in tighter places than this."

137

Looking at him, Woody guessed it was true. Go ahead, he thought. Climb on his horse and ride out, why don't you?

"I don't like this, Ruel."

"Neither do I," Ruel shrugged. "But it's the best we can do. You've got to play the cards that are dealt you."

"I dealt us these cards. If I hadn't gone off half-cocked back there—"

"Water over the dam," Ruel said. "No good dwelling on that now." He waved Woody toward the dun horse. Woody stared at him with mixed gratitude and annoyance.

"Why're you doin' this? Why should you lay your life on the line to give me a chance?"

"Why shouldn't I?" Ruel asked.

"I asked you somethin'," said Woody. "I'm not leavin' till I get an answer."

"My life isn't worth much," Ruel said. "Yours is."

Woody thought about that. "Are you thinkin' of Jean now?" he asked slowly.

Ruel stared into space, lost in reverie. The expression about his eyes had softened at mention of Jean's name. You're in love with her, Woody thought. Same as I am.

Remembering how Jean had reacted to the possibility that Ruel might be dead, Woody felt a wicked jealousy of this tall, self-contained man.

"Why d' you say your life isn't worth much?"

Ruel looked up and said quietly, "I'm a convict. I broke out of Kitannining three years ago."

Woody was silent a moment, considering this information. "Could I ask what you were in for?"

Ruel's hand came up in a gesture of annoyance. "Does it matter?"

"I guess not." Woody felt as if a weight had slid off his shoulders. An escaped convict was no sort of a husband for Jean. All Woody wanted, suddenly, was to be away from here.

While Ruel tied a rope to the sorrel's bridle, Woody climbed aboard the dun horse. As he gathered up the reins, his eyes avoided those of the man on the ground.

"I'll keep them guessing. You'll have a chance, Ruel."

"You better ride," Ruel said.

Woody could hear the clatter of hooves on the ridge now. He rode out, trailing the sorrel. He looked back, as he was turning into a ravine, and saw Ruel standing where he had left him, a hurt man, a man who had to be—in the nature of things—on the verge of exhaustion.

Why don't he fold? Anyone else in his shoes would've collapsed long ago. He acts like he's willin' to take on the whole world. But what chance has he got? He'll be dead in an hour. So'll I, if I don't get a move on.

Woody touched the dun with his spurs.

18

Ruel waited until Woody turned down into the ravine, out of his line of vision, and then he pivoted slowly, taking stock of his position. He could hear them clattering along the ridge, up above there. Why'd I give Woody my horse? He could've held them off while I made a run for it. My nerves are shot, damn it.

He held his hand in front of him, scowling at it until it stopped trembling; then he moved back into a tangle of rocks. Easing down onto his uninjured leg, he drew his gun and checked the loads.

I hope Woody gets out of this. I hope he lives to tell her what happened up here.

He could hear them dropping down off the ridge now. They must have picked up the sign where he and Woody'd turned off into the gully. They'll be here in a couple of minutes. Not much chance of their failing to notice where I reined in and climbed down. Christ, listen to them. You'd think it was a damned army on the way up here.

In a couple of minutes he was going to be dead. It occurred to him that he might not be doing Jean any favor. Woody might not be the one for her.

He could hear them coming, closer now. He drew his gun and laid his finger against the trigger, flattening himself to the ground and lying still, like the hunted animal that he was.

He heard them ride down out of the piñons and halt their horses less than thirty yards from where he lay hidden. He heard Frank Gant say, after a moment, "So they stopped here. What of it?"

"I dunno, Frank. Somethin' peculiar went on here. I can't figure out them prints."

"Why can't you? What's different about them?"

"One set ain't as deep as the other."

"What're you saying? They rode out of here ridin' one horse double, and leadin' the horse with the limp?"

"I dunno. I'd like to study this sign for a—"

"It's gettin' dark. We don't catch them in the next fifteen minutes, we'll lose them. Come on."

Another voice said, "You could leave him here with a couple of the boys, just in case, Frank."

"Just in case what?"

"In case he's onto something."

There was a pause. Frank Gant's voice said at last, grudgingly, "All right, Ace, get at it. Buck, you and Randy stay with him. The rest of us'll keep going. Fire a couple of shots if you need us."

Ruel, from where he lay behind his screen of rocks, could hear Frank and his group ride on. One of the three men left behind said after a moment, "What're you lookin' for, Ace, exactly?"

"Hold it," Ace said. Ruel, in his mind's eye, could see the man frowning self-importantly as he studied the ground.

If he's at all thorough, it won't take him long to discover my footprints. And then they'll smoke me out. He raised his head for a cautious look at them, just in time to see one of them point his gun at the sky and pull trigger, two times.

What had Frank said? Fire a couple of shots if you need us. So they found my footprints. I'm cooked—I'm done for now. When Frank's bunch get back, they'll flush me out quick enough. Picturing how it would be, he thought, Damned if I'm goin' to lie here and wait for it.

He cocked his gun, holding it against his body in an effort to muffle the sound. It clicked. Ruel, cursing his luck, poked his head up.

The man who'd fired those shots at the sky was punching the empty casings out of his gun, preparatory to reloading. His sidekicks snatched at their weapons.

Ruel shot the one who moved first, driving him back and down. He corrected his aim and shot the second man before he could raise his weapon and fire.

141

The third man, interrupted in the act of reloading, snapped the loading gate shut, brought his gun up at Ruel, and squeezed trigger.

His hammer came down on an empty chamber. He swore, and leaped toward the protection of a stone outcrop.

Ruel's gun tracked him briefly, bucked in his hand, emitting flame. The man fell like a bag of potatoes. He rolled down the slope and came to rest against a gnarled piñon.

From around a high shoulder of weathered granite came a shout, and a clatter of hooves. That'll be Frank's bunch. Ruel's eyes gravitated toward the three men he had shot, toward their horses. If I could commandeer myself a horse I might have a chance. I might live to tell my grandkids about this.

Two of the horses, as he ran limping toward them, went skittering off. He got close enough to the third, which was carrying a carbine in a loose-fitting saddle sling, to make a lunging grab at the reins.

He missed, but as the animal snorted and wheeled away, Ruel yanked the carbine out of its scabbard. He levered a cartridge into the breech of the powerful, short-barreled weapon, and lined it up on the first of Frank Gant's men who came charging around the rock shoulder.

Ruel held his breath, and squeezed it out gently. The man grasped at the horn with both hands, and fell in a pitching dive. A second man showed himself, and Ruel knocked him out of the saddle.

"Around here, boys!" he shouted in a high-pitched, excited voice. "We've got him."

A third man, taking that bait, rounded the turn, saw his fallen companions, and reined in as Ruel triggered. Hit in the chest, he fell with desperate cunning into a tangle of brush and rocks at the trailside.

"Hold it, boys," he screamed. "He's got Murph and Albee!"

Ruel was breathing hard, clutching the carbine, waiting for another candidate to come barreling around that outcrop of granite. Keep coming, boys. Who wants the next bullet?

Nobody came. In a silence broken only by the far-off *peent* of a woodcock, and by his own heavy breathing, Ruel returned to his hiding place in the rocks. It had been a busy two minutes.

Five men. Five men dead, plus the one I winged, up in the brush there. Six, if you count the one that got blown up with the dam. Six men. What am I, for God's sake, a butcher?

But that was nice—the way they kept coming and gave me something to shoot at. Wouldn't you think they'd be smarter than that? I wonder who they thought that was yelling at them. I wish I could've got my hands on one of their horses and got out of here. Something tells me I've had all the luck I can hope for.

19

Frank Gant hauled back on the reins, mouth-whipping the blue-roan stallion, bringing the animal to a snorting, hock-rattling halt.

"Matheson's put one over on us," he growled, as his men gathered around him.

"How?" McLouth asked.

"You heard Coley yell," Frank said, "same as I did."

McLouth rubbed his pocked chin. "What're you goin' to do?"

"I'll tell you what I'm *not* goin' to do," Frank said. "I'm not goin' to ride around that bend and give him another duck-soup target to shoot at."

"What makes you so sure it's Matheson, Frank? Couldn't it be the other one? What's his name, Yarmon?"

It had to be Matheson, as Frank saw it. For safety's sake now, he pulled the roan up into a small, shallow gully.

He was sitting slumped in the saddle, chin in hand, trying to settle on a course of action, when Coley Newcomb dragged himself out of the brush below the rock shoulder. Coley's face, normally ruddy, was pale as milky water. There was a spreading red stain on his shirt. He was bleeding at the mouth, Frank saw.

"Help him, Lute." Frank couldn't help thinking, as he gave that order, that Coley was beyond being helped now. "Who shot you, Coley? Who's raisin' all the hell around the rock there?"

Coley, too near the end to manage a shrug, gave a dismal flick of his eyes.

"Do somethin' for me Frank, for God's sake. I'm bleedin' to death."

"Who shot you? Was it Matheson?" Frank asked.

"Water," the hurt man said. "Give me water. I'm burnin' up."

"Where would we find water here on top of the mountain?" Frank asked, with a lift of his shoulders.

"Ain't you goin' to do anything for me?" asked Coley.

Frank looked at him, and he could see Coley Newcomb facing up to the fact that he was going to die. A barely perceptible smile bent the hard, killer's mouth. A bitter bravado gleamed in the pain-glazed eyes.

Frank said, "How'd the rest of the boys make out?"

"They're dead," Coley said in a whisper. "That bastard got hold of Buck's carbine. He don't miss. He hits what he shoots at." Coley coughed. A mixture of blood and saliva trickled from the corner of his mouth, down around his chin. "Funny, ain't it, the way things pan out? Always figgered I'd die in bed."

Lute Springer dropped to his knees beside the dying man. "You want me to say some words for you, Coley?"

"Hell with that."

Lute winced. He went on hopefully, stubbornly, "I could say the Lord's Prayer."

"Get away from me," Coley said. "I never give a damn for religion. I ain't grabbin' no rabbit's foot now." He coughed again. There was a glint in his eyes as he looked up at Lute.

"See you in hell," he said, and his mouth quirked. His eyes closed.

Lute probed for the pulse and looked up, swallowing.

"He's dead, Frank," he said, badly shaken. "Why couldn't he let me say some words for him?"

Frank stared at the dead man. It took guts to die as Coley had died, unregenerate, cursing. Although Frank had killed men, it always unnerved him to see a man die. Times like that you realized your own days were numbered.

"Let's think about the son of a bitch that put that slug in him."

McLouth's eyes held a gleam of sadism. "How we goin' to get at him?"

"We'll drop a loop around him," Frank said. "Berne, that'll be your job."

"What do you want me to do?"

"Pick out five men and come in on him from six points of the compass. Get goin' before it's too dark."

"It's dark now, Frank. How're we goin' to box him in if we can't see him?"

"Your problem," Frank said. "You better remember this man's a dead shot. He's hurt, and he knows we're after his hide. Name your men and get goin'."

Red Coombs stood at Frank's elbow, watching Berne and the men he chose ride away through the gathering darkness.

"You sure that was wise, Frank?" the redheaded man asked.

Frank beetled his brows at the foreman. "What's on your mind?" Red looked down, reluctant to speak.

Frank said, "Those boys know there'd be no percentage for them in running out on me."

"I suppose," said the foreman.

Frank turned toward Lute Springer. Indicating a patch of grass some distance away at the trailside, he said, "Take the horses down there, Lute, and let them fill their bellies. Hobbs can go with you."

McLouth said, "That'll only leave you and Red and me holdin' the fort here, Frank."

"So?"

McLouth held to a disgruntled silence. As Lute and Hobbs led the horses away, Frank said, "What's botherin' you, Harry?"

"Nothin'."

"If I didn't know better, I'd say you were spooking."

"Maybe I am. Look, I'll stand up and trade shots with any man, anytime. But skulkin' around in the dark, wonderin' where the other man's at, ain't my kind ot fightin'."

"All we've got to do is sit tight and make sure he doesn't get past us. Berne and the boys will close in on him soon. And there'll be the end of him."

"He could've changed position," Red put in. "He may be halfway down the mountain."

"He's been shot," Frank said. "You saw some of the

146

blood he lost there at the dam last night. I don't guess he'll be movin' around much."

"He's *been* movin' around pretty good, Frank. He done in five men in less than two minutes."

Frank frowned, and remained silent. Night had fallen as they were talking. A bitter wind skidded down off the ridge and tugged at Frank's clothing, making him shiver. Somewhere down mountain he heard a whippoorwill's call; aside from that there was no other sound except the soughing of the wind.

It was a time for patience. Years ago Frank had read, or been told, that the ancient Arabs, traveling in caravan across the Sahara, had made the dreary hours pass by playing games of chess verbally, outlining moves to one another on an imaginary chessboard.

Now, lying in the dark on the hard ground beside his hired gunhand and his redheaded foreman, Frank amused himself by attempting to recall some of the more memorable poker hands he had been dealt, and how he had bet them. He tired of the exercise after ten minutes, and lay shivering, mentally cursing the drifter.

After what seemed a long time he heard shooting, off somewhere in the darkness.

"That'll be Berne," Frank said with a grin. "One of Berne's gang has probably nailed him."

"Or been nailed by him," McLouth said.

"Whose side you on?" Frank asked.

McLouth didn't answer. They lay shivering for an hour, talking little, and then in whispers. They heard another burst of gunfire.

McLouth said, with a trace of irony, "What was you sayin' an hour ago, Frank?"

"All right. So they missed him the first go round. This time they got him."

"Maybe," McLouth said.

"He can't go on tradin' bullets with our boys without stoppin' one," Frank said. "He's human. He bleeds when he's hit, same as anybody."

"Someone's got to hit him first," Red Coombs put in gloomily.

"Shut up a minute." Frank could hear a horse moving away deliberately through the darkness.

"One of our boys must've had a bellyful," McLouth said.

"Could be Matheson ridin' out," Red said. McLouth snickered, and the foreman said, "I say that's Matheson. I say he's running."

"Do you?" McLouth said.

"Quit it, you two," Frank said. All three of them fell into a gloomy silence. Frank lay on his back, with his crossed arms for a pillow, and occupied his mind by contemplating the sky. In an hour's time the constellations, because of the earth's rotation, appeared to wheel across the heavens.

From somewhere back in the trees came the tinkle of a bit-chain, a pound of hooves, and a blood-curdling yell.

"Hoo-ah-h-h-h!" an all-too-familiar voice shouted. "Git. Git now, you wall-eyed devils!"

"What is it?" Red Coombs said. "Goddamnit, what's happened?"

"I'll say one thing for that drifter," McLouth said in his dry way. "He gets around. He keeps busy."

A shadowy figure emerged from the trees and came running, dodging, across a boulder field toward Frank. It was Lute Springer.

"Get down," Frank hissed, and Lute hit the dirt. He crawled the rest of the way to the mouth of the gully.

"The drifter got Hobbs," he said in reply to Frank's question. "He's drove off all our horses."

Frank swore. "Why didn't you and Hobbs keep your eyes open?"

"We did, Frank. He come up on us out of nowhere. He moves around in the night like some damn big cat. He's as hard to pin down as a shadow."

"What kind of man is he anyway, Frank?" Red asked. "Don't he know we got him outnumbered?"

"He knows."

"Then why don't he act like he knows?" complained the foreman.

Frank, noting how Red's voice quavered, said, "What's the matter with you?"

148

"I'd like to know what's in his mind, that's all. He acts like he ain't right in the head. Where's he come off, takin' on the bunch of us? Why's he drove off our horses? Don't he know there's only one way this can end?" Frank was moodily silent. The redheaded man said, "Maybe he'll run, now he's put us afoot, Frank."

"You think so?"

"Why not?" asked the foreman.

Lute Springer put in his two cents' worth. "He ain't goin' to run. He'll stay till he's killed us. Every one of us."

"Shut up, you fool," Frank said.

"It's the truth." Lute had the bit in his teeth, and was determined to speak his piece. "He'll kill us. Ain't none of us goin' to get off this mountain alive. We're sinners. We sinned against the Lord Jesus. This here's retribution."

"You don't shut your fool mouth, I'll give you retribution."

"He's here on the Lord's business, Frank. He's an avengin' angel come to punish us for the evil we done. You couldn't kill him that first day, hard as you tried. Any other man would've died after a beating like the one you gave him. Reason he didn't die is he was sent here for a purpose, sent by God Almighty."

Lute, as he rattled on, sat up straight and, to accent his points, waved his arms.

"Get your head down," Frank told him.

"The bullet ain't been made that can kill him. He'll do us all in before mornin'."

Frank said, "Get your head down. Move, damn you, when I tell you somethin'."

"Don't use that kind of language on me, Frank."

"I'll use any kind of language I want to. Get down."

"You're a lost, Godless man, Frank. You're goin' to burn. You're goin' to burn in the fire of eternal damnation. There's no way you can save yourself from it."

Frank's gun was in his hand. He brought the heavy, octagonal barrel down and around, striking Lute on the temple. There was a sound of bone crunching. Lute went down smoothly and silently, like a man sliding into water. He didn't cry out or groan or thrash about when he reached the ground.

149

"How is he?" Frank asked, as McLouth checked Lute over.

"He ain't goin' to preach no more sermons."

"Is he dead?"

McLouth's silence was all the answer Frank needed.

Red Coombs said, "You didn't have to hit him that hard, Frank."

"Didn't I?"

"He'd've been one more gun for us, for that drifter to silence."

"He wasn't any good to us, the shape he was in."

"So there's three of us now," said the foreman. "A dozen and more of us, set out on a manhunt, and now there's only three of us left."

"What's the matter, Red?" McLouth jeered. "You missin' your mother?"

"I don't like the way this is goin'."

"There's three of us, like you said. The odds're three to one in our favor."

"Three to one odds ain't nothing," Red said. "Not when the one moves around in the dark like a cat."

"Keep your voices down," Frank said. He was on the lookout for some sign of the drifter. "Work your way over there toward the trees, boys. Dig yourselves in over there. Keep your eyes open and your guns handy."

"What's the idea?" McLouth asked.

"Matheson's had his share of luck. I've got a feelin' it's our turn to get lucky."

"But why—"

"Goddamnit, don't argue with me," Frank said. "Get goin'."

As McLouth and the foreman went skulking off, Frank's hand moved exploringly along Lute Springer's leg until it reached the dead man's hip holster. It was empty. Frank lay back, a grim humor twisting his mouth as he realized McLouth had helped himself to Lute's gun.

Maybe he ought to have staked Red out over there in the trees, and kept McLouth, who never seemed to miss a trick, with him here in the gully. But Frank had wanted to play a lone hand. If it comes down to me and the drifter,

I can handle him, Frank thought. I might not have to handle him. McLouth may finish him off first.

Frank turned over soundlessly, cursing the cold, and warmed his gun hand under his arm. From time to time he took it out and flexed his fingers.

An hour dragged by, during which the air seemed to grow steadily colder. He lay in misery, thinking what he would do to that drifter if he could get his hands on him.

He heard a small sound close by. He drew breath and held it, lying still, gun in hand, ready.

"Frank?" It was McLouth, speaking in a whisper out of the near darkness.

"Here." As the gunman crawled toward him, Frank said, "Where's—"

"Red's done for, Frank. Matheson got him."

Frank felt as if he had been struck in the pit of the stomach. "How? I didn't hear any—"

"He must've jumped him and used a knife on him, is all I can figure. I couldn't see what was goin' on. I'd sent Red out to reconnoiter, and—"

"You sent him out? Goddamnit, what for? If you'd stuck together one of you might have nailed the drifter."

McLouth didn't comment for a moment. Then he said, "How come the three of us never stuck together?"

"Go on," Frank said. "You were saying you sent him out to reconnoiter. Then what?"

"All I know is what I heard. He let out one of them huffing grunts, like he'd been jumped by a bobcat. I laid there still as a stone for a half hour, then started to worm my way back an inch at a time. I never moved except when the moon was hid by a cloud."

"You've turned pretty cautious, haven't you. Harry?"

"Sure."

"Why?"

"That man's a damn cat, Frank."

Frank was absently fingering the specimen of coal in his pocket. The man in the moon peered out at him from behind a cloud, and a thousand stars stared down accusingly at him. I wish I hadn't killed Lute, he thought. Funny how that religious crap'll make a man like him brave. He sure read me off before I bashed his brains in. What was it he said? "You'll burn, Frank. You'll burn in the fire of eternal damnation."

"Maybe it's time we changed our tactics," Frank murmured.

"How?"

Frank took a moment to think. "Matheson seems to have a talent for finding his way around in the dark. We've played into his hands. We'd better postpone the showdown till morning."

"You mean lay out here the rest of the night without no slicker, or even a blanket between us and the ground?"

"That's right."

"Hell."

"I don't like it any more than you do," Frank said. "I don't think we'll suffer too much. We have one advantage over that drifter."

"What's that?"

"There's two of us. We can keep each other warm. Who'll be in better shape for the showdown, come morning? Us, or that drifter?"

"Goin' to be a long night, Frank."

"For him. Don't forget he stopped a bullet last night. He's been on the go pretty much ever since. He must be chilled to the marrow."

Frank took the coal from his pocket, so that he would not have to lie on it, and rolled over against the gunfighter. McLouth seemed to be made up of protruding shoulder blades and bony sharp elbows. The man smelled like an old wet boot held too close to the fire. It was all Frank could do not to shudder.

He thought of Matheson out there somewhere in the dark, with no one to talk to, no one to help him keep warm, and snuggled closer to the gunfighter.

152

20

Ruel lay shivering, hidden in jackpines at the foot of a granite ledge. He took little comfort from the carpet of pine needles that cushioned him and insulated him from the ground.

Blood was seeping from the bullet wound in his leg. The bleeding had started again an hour ago, when he'd jumped Frank Gant's foreman. He could remember, too clearly, how that had been. The Y Lightning man had grunted and started to struggle, then had gone suddenly limp as Ruel's blade found his vital organs.

Trying to get his mind off that now, Ruel ripped off part of his shirt and folded it against his wound. His teeth were chattering. Everything he did seemed to be too great an effort. He had never felt so cold, or so tired. It was the blood he had lost, he supposed, that made him mind the cold so much.

He chafed his hands, and cupped them to his mouth, blowing on them. What'll I do an hour from now? Somehow, despite the fact he was suffering miserably from the cold, despite the fact he was almost too weak to stand, he must remain wide awake and alert.

Above him, against the night sky, he could trace out the dim silhouette of the ridge. The moon had heeled down on the other side of the mountain, leaving this side in darkness.

Wonder how many's left up there? I ran off nine or ten horses. I've knocked off pretty near that many men, in the past three, four hours. I'd say there's two left. Three at the most.

He shivered again, and tucked his head down into the

collar of his brush-popper jacket. I need a fire, he thought. He lay there in the dark thinking about it. In his imagination he built himself a fire. He could see the yellow flames licking upward from the blackened wood that they fed on; he could hear his fire hissing and cracking, almost feel the warmth from it.

He heard a dead branch groan; he heard a pine cone rattle as it danced in the wind. Now, in the dark and in the cold, he remembered the men he had killed. He had branded himself by this night's work. From now on he would be known as a killer.

It was them or me, he thought. They set out to hunt me down, and I turned on them. But all those men, Jesus!

I wonder what Frank's doin' now. I wish he'd come down here—him and whoever's still with him—and have his try at me. They don't soon come, I'll be froze solid.

He flexed his fingers, and rubbed up circulation in his arms and in his one good leg.

Several times, as the air grew colder, he caught himself dozing, and had to pinch himself to stay awake. It would have helped if he could get up and move about, uncramp his muscles. To do so, he knew, would be playing into the hands of the men up the slope who were out to kill him.

Frank knows how it is for me, Ruel thought. He'll wait me out, damn him. He won't make his move until morning.

The longer he thought about it, the surer he was that he had guessed the other man's game. If he could be dead sure he might risk a catnap. He'd never last until sunrise unless he got some rest. But what if he failed to awaken?

He gave a moment's grim thought to that possibility, and to its implications; then, using his knife, he scooped out a shallow trench for his body, burrowed down into it, and covered himself with pine needles.

It was a makeshift arrangement but it kept the wind off him, it helped his body retain its own heat. Now, warning himself against sleeping too soundly, telling himself he must be awake and ready for anything when the sun rose, he shut his eyes and relaxed.

His eyes fluttered open as the sky was beginning to

154

lighten eastward. For a panicky instant he was afraid he had slept too long. He moved his arms experimentally under their covering of pine needles and sat up creakily, feeling a thousand years old.

While he was uncramping himself he heard a footfall. Sitting perfectly still, with just his eyes moving, with his heart going thump, thump, thump in his chest, he watched a buck deer pick its way daintily down a game trail. A gray chipmunk darted across an open space between trees, and scurried into a tangle of rocks.

Ruel eased back onto an elbow, sighing, feeling a fluttery weakness inside.

As the new day's light strengthened, birds became active. A pair of crows cawed at one another somewhere down the mountain. A jay scolded raucously. The crows flew toward Ruel now, heading for a dead tree—one of those old sentinel pines that doesn't look complete without a crow or two perching on it.

The crows veered away before they reached the pine and flew off at a tangent, cawing shrilly. Ruel knew all he needed to know then. Why wait for it? he thought. He checked his gun over, taking his time, and feeling unexpectedly calm. In some strange way he was detached from the harsh reality of this situation, as though his mind were standing off to one side observing what was happening to his body.

He holstered his gun and began to move cautiously, laboriously up the slope.

He had gone forty yards, keeping low, taking advantage of all available cover, when he heard the sound. He lay behind an imbedded rock, something inside of him tightening, twisting. All right, here it comes, he thought. He flexed the fingers of his right hand.

A man's head moved out from behind an upthrust of granite. It was Harry McLouth, pulling himself along the ground by the leverage of his elbows. The gunman's eyes kept flicking about. They flicked past Ruel, then came darting back.

Shock held the man momentarily rooted. "Mornin'," Ruel said in a cool dry voice. He saw McLouth go for his

155

gun. He brought his own gun up stiffly, too slowly, and squeezed a trigger which seemed to him to have frozen in place and did not want to trip.

He saw McLouth's gun coming up at him, and told himself bitterly that he had not been in time. I'm dead, he thought, and then his gun was kicking in his hand. He saw McLouth's body jerk to the impact of the slug, saw the utter disbelief in the gunman's eyes as he slumped down.

McLouth was still trying to get his gun up. It was too heavy for him. He dropped the gun and rolled down the slope and lay still.

Frank Gant, farther up the slope, had stepped out from behind a tree. He snapped a shot out. Ruel, sagging to one knee, shot hurriedly, hitting Frank in the shoulder, twisting him half around, and forcing him to take cover behind another tree.

Only Frank's buttocks, the soft, well-padded buttocks of a man who had earned his living at the card tables, remained visible to Ruel.

Ruel took deliberate aim and pressed it out, stinging Frank, rousing his temper. He stepped out into the open, lifting his gun, and Ruel shot again, hitting him in the chest. Frank caught at the tree for support, scraping bark off it, and fell to his knees.

Using only one hand—his left hand was clenched—he tried to get his gun up for a shot at Ruel. It was too much effort. He sagged against the tree, fell sideways, and lay quivering for a moment.

Ruel went up and knelt beside Frank's suddenly motionless body. He pried something hard, shiny, and black out from between Frank's fingers. For an instant he stared down uncomprehendingly at the dead man, then he turned away, his eyes crinkling with sardonic amusement.

He had turned too quickly. He had to sit on a rock and prop his head in his hands to keep from fainting. He was still sitting there twenty minutes later, barely conscious, when he heard the unmistakable clatter of steel-shod hooves against unyielding stone. His eyes darted about, seeking cover.

He made it halfway down to the jackpines before he keeled over.

156

He came to in the girl's bed at the C Bar. She entered the room when he called, and said in response to Ruel's question: "Woody brought you in, on a travois. You've been here the better part of two days. Could you keep some broth down, do you think?"

"I'm hungry enough," Ruel said with a serious expression, "to eat that bedpost."

Jean said later, as she spooned broth into his mouth, "Dad's had a mining expert look at those coal deposits up on the mountain. He's in town with Woody, dickering with a syndicate that wants to mine the coal on a royalty basis. It looks as if our troubles are over. Dad's thinking of buying Y Lightning."

"Y Lightning?"

"Mrs. Gant owns it now," Jean said. "She's next-of-kin, and Frank didn't have any will. He probably thought he'd live forever. She has no use for the place, Ruel. She's going back East, to her grandchildren. She's better off, thanks to you. So is everyone in this part of the country. You should hear the tongues wagging about you in town."

All I want, Ruel thought, is to go my own way. The less notice people take of me, the better. When the girl left the room, Ruel eased himself gingerly out of her bed and fumbled into his clothes. He limped out to the kitchen, where Jean sat shelling peas.

"I'm ridin' out."

"But you can't, the condition you're in, Ruel. I—I won't let you."

She followed him across the yard to the corral, and watched him make two unsuccessful attempts to swing his saddle onto the dun.

"I won't help you, Ruel. This is sheer folly."

He set himself on his good leg and tried again, making it this time. As he tightened cinch, the ground began to swirl and he had to lean against the dun to keep from falling. The girl came over to him.

"Won't you stay, Ruel?"

"I'm afraid I can't afford to."

"You mean—because the authorities will come after

you?" Ruel looked at her in surprise. "Dad's told me your story."

"He shouldn't have," Ruel said. "He had no right."

"He felt he had no right *not* to tell me."

He wanted to ask her what she meant by that. Instead, he climbed heavily to the saddle.

"You don't have to run all your life, Ruel. They might let you off easier than you think, if you went back. There's hardly a soul hereabouts who wouldn't put in a word for you. All those character references—"

"I'm not goin' back." He had that lonesome, achey feeling in the throat as he touched the dun with his boot heels.

Jean called after him, "Would it make any difference if I told you I love you?"

Ruel reined in. Something seemed to be swelling up in his chest, making it hard to breathe. He was afraid to look around, afraid of what he might see in Jean's eyes—of what it might do to his feelings.

"Ruel, stay. Stay till you're strong enough to go back and serve out your time. I'll wait. I'd wait twenty years, if I had to."

As he turned to look at her, he could feel his jaw sagging. "You sayin' you'd marry me?"

"Yes, darling. Yes."

"What about Woody?"

"I'm not promised to Woody. Even if I were, he'd never hold me to it. Not after what you did for him up there on the mountain."

"I'm not the man for you," Ruel said.

"You are, Ruel. You are. You're more man than you've ever let yourself realize. I'll wait. Can't you understand that I *want* to wait, darling?"

Ruel sat there in a warm, pleasant confusion. I better get out of here. I'm not for her. Or am I? he wondered. I can't be such a bad sort, not if a girl like her is willin' to marry me, knowin' what she knows about me.

Jean smiled at him uncertainly now. Ruel grasped the horn and stepped down. He had found his place. There would be no more running.

A NOVEL AS BIG AS LIFE

THE GREAT SANTINI

PAT CONROY

He's animal, devastating, and utterly real. He's like someone every one of us knows. He's the ultimate in machismo, the charming redneck, the consummate brute. He's the man you hate to love—but you will.

"A fine, funny, brawling book."

The National Observer

"Robust and vivid . . . full of feeling."   *Newsday*

"An impressive novel."   *San Francisco Examiner*

 Avon/32680/$1.95   (TINI 6-77)